Between the Lines

Between the Lines

Edited By

Michael Knost

Editor: Michael Knost

Published by Seventh Star Press, LLC.

ISBN Number: 978-1-941706-49-7

Seventh Star Press
www.seventhstarpress.com
info@seventhstarpress.com

Printed in the United States of America

First Edition

Table of Contents

Introduction by Michael Knost...1

Acts by Elizabeth Gaucher...3

The Fifth Patient by Trace Conger..13

Sleep Driving by Angela Lambert..25

The Fall of Sleep by J. Mace...37

Got to Keep Moving by Katherine Sanger....................................49

Jumping In by C.J. Brooks..59

Stardust by Ben Eads..65

Purple Eclipse by Cynthia Dawn Griffen....................................77

Fixing a Broken Shadow by Marty Young....................................87

Playtime's End by Nicole E. Castle...97

Rattle and Sway by B.D. Prince...105

Intellectual Property by Lynn Butcher.......................................119

His Flower, His Treasure by Kenneth W. Cain...........................129

The Painted Universe by Lee E. E. Stone..................................139

Worlds Hath No Chance Against a Woman Scorned by Roxanne Crouse....151

Soaked in Blood by Denise Wyant...161

Kindlestorm's Anomalous Adventure, by LRH Rendell-Hayes....171

Introduction

What you are about to read is the result of the most difficult anthology I have ever produced. And it's not because of the writers or their work, it is because I suffer from clinical depression and I battled some of my worst bouts during every stage of this project.

What should have taken months to complete, took years.

Some writers didn't understand, and I certainly do not blame them. Unless you have suffered the dark tendrils of depression, you can't understand. So, to the wonderful participating writers, thank you for your patience, and to those who lost their patience, thank you for not skewering me.

This anthology is nothing like anything I have ever edited before. But it's something I've always wanted to do. And I am so glad I did.

It all started with an idea for an online writing class I was conducting. I gave the students an opening sentence and a closing sentence and asked them to write a story *Between the Lines*. And, yes, everyone received the very same lines.

That means every story opens with:

"Kelvin pressed against the wound as blood seeped around

his hands."

And ends with:

"Watching the train disappear into the night, he brought the flower to his nose before tossing it to the tracks."

I was amazed that each writer created a completely different story, with completely different characters, all with the same beginning and ending. And as a writing teacher, I am so proud of the quality of the stories. In fact, I predict many of the writers, should they refuse to give up the ghost, will find their names on the covers of many future anthologies, magazines, and novels.

Now, prepare yourself for the wonders you'll find *Between the Lines*.

Michael Knost
August, 2016

Acts

by Elizabeth Gaucher

Kelvin pressed against the wound as blood seeped around his hands. The dream was always the same, though the woman in bed next to him rarely was. He was to the point where he could be almost conscious within his own night terrors, having a sense of another lover's impending departure before he even woke. He felt his eyes fly open to the white light of morning and realized he was staring at the dirty wall. The sheet wrapped tight to his shoulder, cold and damp. He squeezed his eyes shut and sighed. Exhaustion was his only loyal companion, never gone for long and always guaranteed to come back for a long visit should Kelvin hope for too long.

"I hate you," emerged from his lips. "I really hate you."

"Hey. Hi. Good morning to you, too." The voice came from across the room.

Dear God. She's still here.

Kelvin sat up, careful to demonstrate strength and speed but not panic. A large invisible cotton ball filled his mouth and he wondered when he could speak. The night before was a sketch with disconnected lines. His walks around downtown tended to be in search of open doors, anywhere, and those doors often led to too much caffeine. The goal was to remain conscious as long as possible to stave off the dream, but occasionally he caved and walked into bars. Last night had been an alcohol night.

Pushing the sheet back to his waist, he turned to the voice. A woman sat calmly, her legs tucked under her in an overstuffed chair. Her nearly black purple toenails gleamed against her pale skin, and Kelvin's gaze fell on a cluster of tattooed flower blossoms at her ankle. She pulled a rubber band out of her jeans pocket and lifted layers of dark blonde hair into a ponytail. She suddenly looked much younger than Kelvin remembered. Last night she had worn heavy eye makeup and now her face was clean. He wanted to say something to her, but he couldn't form a sentence.

Kelvin looked with sadness at the stacks of newspapers surrounding his visitor's chair. He had taken to saving the papers for exactly fifty days at a time, then reading each one in its entirety before burning them all methodically by date in a metal trashcan in the yard behind the apartments. This little obsessive compulsion soothed his psyche like nothing else since the bleeding started.

Today was burning day. Hopefully everything was still in order.

"You like to hang onto things, don't you?" his visitor asked. When Kelvin refused a reply, she lobbed another starter. "Who do you hate?" she asked. "I hope it's not me. Whoever it is, I'm pretty sure I didn't do it. I haven't had enough time." She laughed then and reddened a little, "Can I get you a glass of water or something?" Skewse, West Virginia, produced a unique accent in most locals and Kelvin did not hear it in her words.

He found his voice. "Listen…it's not you. I'm not used to anyone being here when I wake up is all." He paused, scanning the room for any other surprises. The woman was across the efficiency now to the sink. She moved like a ballet dancer, her jeans and thin red T-shirt in odd contrast to her elegant, fluid steps and arm sweeps.

Handing him a tumbler of ice water, she looked into his face. Her eyes held an unexpected gentleness. He accepted the water.

For the first time in months, Kelvin felt the knot in his belly soften slightly.

In the back yard, the trash barrel stood ready and waiting for his ritual and he wondered how soon the stranger would show herself out. Instead of leaving, the woman sat back in the chair. Aging sentinels of yellowing newspapers surrounded her position, almost daring Kelvin to address their presence. His visitor let one delicate hand rest on the nearest pile of pulp, fingering the edges of yesterday's news. When she spoke, her tone was kind but serious.

"Tell me what happens at night."

The next sixty seconds felt endless, as Kelvin looked through the woman and formulated his answer. No one had ever asked him what happened at night. People just left.

"Why do you want to know?" His voice on edge, he felt anger and then a sudden surrender. "No, it doesn't matter. I'll tell you." There was only so long he could hold it all. If someone was willing to hear it, he was willing to tell it.

His hands in his hair, Kelvin rubbed his scalp with a slow rhythm and turned his head away as he spoke. "I have dreams, hallucinations really." He paused, refocusing his thoughts. "No, I have *one* dream. There is always someone or something bleeding. Sometimes the bleeding is profuse. Sometimes it is slow, but it's always steady. I try to stop the blood but every time I wake up before I know if I stopped it." Kelvin looked back at the woman in the chair. Her eyes were heavy but intent.

"I used to have that dream," she said. "But I don't anymore. I can help you."

Kelvin felt the knot return. What was she talking about, she used to have that dream? She must be crazy. No one could help him. Why did he ever think this was a good idea? "I doubt it," he said flatly. He could see she was not going to leave on her own and he began to regret leaving his apartment, ever. "Look, I don't know you. I don't know why you are still here, I don't know why you are here at all. I don't know why you think you can help me or why you even care. I want you to go now please. It's nothing personal. You seem really nice but it's time for you to go."

The woman reached for her shoes. "There is a church down the tracks from here. If you walk from The Dovetail pub for five miles south, you will find it in the woods off to the right. You should go there."

Lifting her faded denim jacket from the back of a ladder-back chair she floated past Kelvin to the door. He realized he hadn't expected her to leave without hesitation. "Thanks for staying. Thanks for talking. This is not a good time for me. I'm sorry," he managed to say as she put her hand on the doorknob.

Stopping in the open doorway, the woman spoke with her back to Kelvin. "My sister died in her sleep when I was a teenager. We'd had an argument the day before. I went to sleep thinking I would tell her I was sorry in the morning." She raised her head and said, "That's when my dream started, the night after she died. There was always this bleeding, I couldn't stop it."

Kelvin drew air into his chest and let it go with difficulty. "You said the dream did stop, though."

She turned to face him. "Yes. It did. After fifty consecutive nights of the same dream, it stopped."

Kelvin stared. He almost wasn't breathing at all now. At last he said, "The church?"

"Yes," was all she said and then she was gone.

***

Regaining focus took time. Kelvin sank into his reading chair and contemplated his newspaper stacks. The upholstery emitted a subtle flowery scent, the only evidence of his overnight visitor's real presence in the room. Dry leaves crackled and scraped as they swept past the window. Large gusts of wind threatened his burning project but thoughts of the place in the woods five miles out of town overrode concern for his ritual.

After fifty consecutive nights of the same dream, it stopped.

The wind was at his back as he pulled a thick wool collar close to his throat. Five miles on foot was a hike, but his footsteps seemed effortless with the urgent air behind him. He hadn't been aware there was a church this close to town. The trappings of faith and a spiritual life were for children and adults with simple minds. Rarely had Kelvin encountered anything religious that did more than enrage or bore him.

The woman from the night before, however, intrigued him.

He did not remember bringing her back to the apartment, though he must have. How else could she have been there? A larger question swirled in his brain. Why did she stay? He could not shake the feeling that she came as a messenger. Once she had told him about the church she was gone. She left with complete comfort and ease as if her work was done.

After about three miles of walking, he sat down on the cold iron tracks. He had to pull himself together. Turning his head to his right he saw the long narrow path he had traveled to this point. He stared for several minutes into the nothingness, wind gusts chafing his face. He held his face in his hands and pressed his fingers hard into his forehead. When he stood up he did not look back again, but pushed forward to the place where dreams stopped and life began.

And then there it was.

Gently curtained by juniper branches, a white wooden church peeked out of the wooded area about fifty yards from the tracks. Kelvin turned instinctively toward the building and stepped with caution toward the tree line. The ground under his feet felt odd, and looking down, he saw a change in the terrain. It was as if hundreds of people had stopped, turned, and moved at this exact point. Where there had been only the train tracks to guide him, there was now a well-trod footpath.

Kelvin swept back the evergreen arms and stepped into the churchyard, then drew a sharp breath at the sight before him. "Why are they _here?_" he whispered. Dozens of gravestones stood between Kelvin and the church door. He remembered churchyards from his boyhood, but never one with the dead anywhere but to the side of the House of the Lord. Nausea crept up into his throat as he imagined walking over the graves to the front door. This had to be a misunderstanding. He tried to walk around the stones, hoping for a side entrance, but the headstones entirely encircled the church. He saw doors on every side of the building, but no path clear of graves.

The sun was starting to set. Kelvin understood he had only one option, to move ahead, but it was difficult to put one foot in front of the other. He focused his gaze on a gravestone halfway between himself and a church entrance. Swirling botanical images were carved in dark grey granite, and limp white flowers rested on the earth beneath the stone. With a halfway point to the door defined, he set off toward the church. He wanted to read the words on the headstone, but fear that they might make him turn back kept him moving. _I'll get it on my way out of here._

The woman's tattooed ankle crossed his mind as he picked up his pace and strode, not looking back, into the little place of worship.

The sanctuary was empty and still. An unlit candle was on the altar, and a stained glass window illuminated by the now-sinking sun showed an image of a crucified Jesus bleeding in his mother's arms. Kelvin winced in pain and looked away to the back of the church. He walked to the last pew, turned, and sat down slowly. He closed his eyes, and felt deep sobs gathering in his chest. He felt tricked. There was nothing here but pain. Why had he listened to a stranger? Why did he allow himself to believe? The bleeding would never end, it was everywhere, and he cursed himself for being so stupid as to believe it could stop. The encroaching darkness was salt in the wound, as soon he would have to sleep and there would be no escape. He sat still, and with all of his strength opened his eyes for the walk out.

The candle on the altar was lit. Growing faint, Kelvin realized he was not breathing and shouted, "Who is here? Show yourself!"

Voices came from every corner of the sanctuary.

"Me voila."

"Ich bin hier."

"Hinneni".

"Lo sono qui."

Kelvin was shaking so hard he could barely walk, but he wanted to run. He wanted to blow out of this place harder and faster than the wind that whipped through the door at the back of the sanctuary carrying thousands of white flower petals with it over the altar and up to the gleaming stained glass like a carnival's celebration. Looking up, he froze. The window's image had changed.

The Christ stood now whole, his wounds healed, and his earthly family around him in adoration. Suspended over the scene was a white dove. Stunned by the window's transformation, Kelvin stopped running long enough to hear a voice he recognized.

"Here I am."

Not possible. Not possible. This is a trick.

Unable to stop himself, Kelvin turned in the direction of his son's voice. Standing in the back of the church was a slight six-year-old boy with windswept blonde hair and sparkling eyes. Through his tears Kelvin scanned the tiny form for bullet wounds. His brain burst at the seams with repressed pain. He remembered his son, shot to death by a disturbed man in a random act of violence. Years ago...over thirty years ago. Yet he was here. He was whole. There was no bleeding.

"Dylan, son, my God. Is that really you?"

"Yes, Daddy. It is me. It is really all of us."

A chorus of voices swelled into the words, "Here we are." Turning to the altar, Kelvin saw hundreds of children's faces looking at him kindly from every corner and every wall of the church. They were boys and girls, toddlers and teenagers, light and dark, large and small. Every child held a white flower.

Memories crashed out of Kelvin's mind in a torrential mix of pain and relief. The school at 5050 Shepherds Lane. Dylan's collection of fifty toy soldiers that he kept orderly and at attention on shelves in his room. Fifty dollars he had in his pocket, saved to buy his mother a necklace for her 50th birthday, the day the police car pulled up in front of his house. Fifty rounds of ammunition.

"Daddy." The word pulled Kelvin back to Dylan's image.

"Daddy, touch me. Then tell the others, okay? We are here, and we are waiting."

Kelvin reached out his arms for his child, and felt the warmth of a living body against his own. "I don't know how to let go," he gasped.

"We are all waiting, Daddy. You have work to do. Tell the others. Your work makes us whole."

Kelvin looked into his child's eyes. "Yes," was all he said.

Though it took all of his capacity to leave the church, he did so. Passing the gravestone he'd ignored on the way in he paused to read these words surrounded by engraved Columbine blossoms:

> *I will pour out my Spirit on all people.*
> *Your sons and daughters will prophesy,*
> *your young men will see visions,*
> *your old men will dream dreams. – Acts 2:17*

The path back to the train tracks was well worn, and this time it gave Kelvin comfort. He felt a small bulge in his coat's breast pocket and slipped a hand inside to feel the silky blossoms of a strong flower. A long train rattled from behind him and headed towards home.

Watching the train disappear into the night, he brought the flower to his nose before tossing it to the tracks.

About the author: Elizabeth Gaucher is a writer, editor, and creator. A West Virginia native living in Middlebury, Vermont, she is also a woman living with multiple sclerosis for nearly two decades. Her essays have appeared in *Mud Season Review, Pithead Chapel, Still: The Journal,* and more. Her website, www.elizabethgaucher.com, lists more publication and work. She holds a Master of Fine Arts (MFA) degree from WV Wesleyan College. She is also the founder and editor of the online literary magazine, *Longridge Review.*

The Fifth Patient

by Trace Conger

Kelvin pressed against the wound as blood seeped around his hands. He pierced the suture needle into the pale skin next to the incision and withdrew it on the other side.

Dr. Mueller supervised while Fleetwood Mac played over the operating room's speakers.

I don't want to know the reasons why love keeps right on walking down the line.

"Nice work, Kelvin. Keep those stitches tight," said Dr. Mueller.

Kelvin continued until he closed the wound and tied off the last suture. He set the needle driver on the surgical tray with a clank and stepped back to admire his handiwork.

"Nice job, everyone," said Dr. Mueller. "It's never easy having one of our own on the table."

Now you tell me that I'm crazy. That's nothing that I didn't know.

With a nod from Dr. Mueller, a nurse wheeled the gurney through the operating room doors, taking nine-year-old Isabel Sanger to recovery.

***

Dr. Peter Sanger knocked over two picture frames and an empty coffee cup reaching for the ringing phone on his desk.

"Isabel's out of the O.R.," said the voice on the other end. "She did great in surgery, but a fluid test came back positive for a bacterial infection. I'm starting her on antibiotics and want to keep monitoring for sepsis."

"Sepsis?"

"Just as a precaution, but I do want to keep her in the hospital until the infection clears. Once she wakes up, they're taking her to room ten-fifty-three. Should be about an hour."

"Ten-fifty-three? Thank you." Sanger scribbled the number on his notepad and hung up the phone.

His little girl, who just yesterday was dressed in her green and gold soccer uniform, was now draped in a surgical gown, a three-inch incision where her appendix used to be. He exhaled and closed his eyes.

A knock startled him.

"The hospital's no place for a child," said the man in the doorway. He wore a gray suit and hat that were as anemic as the army of white coats roaming the hospital hallways.

The tall man looked out of place, but Sanger couldn't identify the specific quality that made him appear that way. Maybe it was his pale skin. Not albino pale, but a complexion that suggested he spent more time indoors than out. Or, maybe it was the way he stood with his body cocked to one side, like he was leaning on a cane that wasn't there.

He held a manila folder and had a small green pencil tucked behind his right ear. Sanger recognized it as the same type of pencil that littered the pockets of his golf bag.

"Appendectomy wasn't it?" said the tall man.

"Excuse me?"

"Your daughter, Isabel. She came through surgery all right?"

14

The man hobbled toward the desk like a praying mantis moving across a wet car hood.

"Can I help you with something?"

"Sorry. Betty wasn't at her desk, and I saw the door was open. I have a one-thirty appointment." He reached out his hand. "Wallace Harper."

"Are you a pharma rep? We no longer allow reps on campus. If you want to meet with a physician, you'll have to schedule time with their individual offices."

"I thought all pharma reps were nice-looking blonds with big tits," said Wallace lowering his hand. "Unfortunately, I don't fit the profile." He took a seat and used both of his hands to lift his left leg over his right. Then he sat back, removed his hat, and placed it on his bent knee. This was the most natural the man had looked since walking into Sanger's office.

"I'm here to meet the new chief of staff. You replaced Dr. Connolly, correct?"

"That's me." Sanger motioned to the stack of file boxes in the corner of his office. "And I'm slammed playing catch up. I can give you five minutes."

"That's all I need." Wallace slid the manila folder across the desk. "That's for you."

Sanger pulled a packet from the folder and riffled through it. "This is the hospital's patient list. Where did you get it?"

"It'd be tough to do my job without it." Wallace steadied his hat and uncrossed his legs with the same effort it took to cross them. He leaned forward and reached for his ID, which was attached to a retractable cord that made a zipping sound as he pulled it from his hip. Wallace held it up like a detective flashing his badge at a crime scene.

Sanger stared at the fading headshot that resembled every DMV photo ever taken. WALLACE HARPER, BUREAU OF AGING AND MORTALITY.

"Bureau of Aging and Mortality?" said Sanger rising from his chair. "If that's some kind of joke, I don't have time for it."

"Every week fifty-one-thousand-nine-hundred-and-twenty-three people die in the United States," said Wallace. "Twenty-six-thousand-five-hundred-and-twenty-seven of those individuals die in hospitals. Northwestern Memorial Hospital, your facility, is responsible for an average of five deaths every week."

Sanger sank back into his chair. "I don't know what you're insinuating, but our medical staff does everything they can to give every patient the care they need—"

"Save your speech," said Wallace. "Patients die in hospitals every day. That's not a reflection of the care you provide or the skill of your medical staff. It's simply a fact of life. People get sick, they go to hospitals, and some of these individuals die. I'm not here to assign blame."

"Then why are you here?"

"I'm your mortality representative, Dr. Sanger. I'm here to schedule your deaths for the week. Five of them."

"To schedule my deaths? Have you lost your goddamn mind?"

"I understand this is an unusual conversation, but I assure you my mental faculties are intact."

"You're not doing much to convince me of that."

"Dr. Sanger, you can't possibly comprehend the administrative burden of managing the deaths of thousands of people every week. I'm responsible for all hospital mortalities in the Chicago and Great Lakes Region."

"And you plan on killing five people in this hospital?" Sanger glanced at his watch and slid his hand closer to the telephone.

"No, that's another department." Wallace rolled his eyes. "I only manage the process. For every hospital in the Chicago—"

"And the Great Lakes Region," Sanger said. "I got that part. So, you're telling me you believe you're somehow responsible for who lives and dies at this hospital?"

"Yes, but so are you."

"How's that?" said Sanger.

"You're responsible for giving me those five names. Those five patients who aren't going to make it through the week. I'll arrange the rest."

"Let's pretend for a moment that I don't think you're batshit crazy. Please explain how, as a doctor who's spent every day of the last twenty-seven years dedicated to saving lives, I'd agree to, essentially, help you kill five people."

"Because I don't know anything about the patients in this hospital, but you do." Wallace edged forward in his chair and tapped the patient list on Sanger's desk with a pale finger. "You know who's close to punching out. Who's on his fourth heart attack. Who's about to lose their battle with cancer. They're just names to me. But to you, they're medical histories. It would be irresponsible for you not to give me the names. Otherwise, I'd just be picking patients at random."

"And these patients, these names I'd give you, they would just up and die tomorrow?"

"No. Five patients dropping dead at the same time would be peculiar."

"Right, because the rest of your story sounds perfectly normal."

"We work on averages," said Wallace. "Each patient will die individually at some point in the next seven days. Sometimes longer. It all evens out in the end."

Sanger checked his watch again and decided he'd been courteous enough. "Well, Wallace, as entertaining as this conversation has been, I'm going to have to ask you to leave now. I've got a hospital to run."

"Dr. Connolly threw me out of this same office twelve years ago," Wallace said. "But he came around after we took five newborns from the nursery the following week. Almost triggered a

Department of Health investigation. So many babies dying at the same time in the same hospital. Horrible thing. Of course, he didn't have a daughter on the tenth floor. You might want to get on board sooner."

Sanger slammed his hand on his desk, knocking the two picture frames even closer to the edge. "Get out!"

Wallace exhaled. He placed his hat back on his head, struggled out of the chair and limped toward the door. "Give me the names by eight o'clock tomorrow evening and the right people die, Dr. Sanger. I'll be back tomorrow for your list. And then every Friday after that."

Sanger followed Wallace to the door and watched him walk down the hallway, keeping one hand on the wall to brace himself. He was about to go back to his desk, when Wallace turned around.

"One more thing. I have to fill your quota with people from the hospital. Once they walk out of here, they're out of my jurisdiction and they're no good to me."

Sanger closed his door, making sure the sound echoed down the hall.

***

A large white envelope teetered on the top of Sanger's swelling inbox. He hadn't noticed it before. Betty must have delivered the mail while he was at lunch. The envelope seemed to tilt towards him and then back again, teasing him to open it. A voice in his head suggested he leave it for later, but he reached for it anyway.

Inside were dozens of post-it notes. Small yellow squares, each with a date and a list of names. Clumps of them, stuck together with sticky post-it adhesive. He grabbed a few from the gummy pile.

8/12/11: William Steinberg, Peter Shea, Christopher Robbins, Sally Mathers, Kathy Melendez

6/17/11: Benjamin Fischer, Edgar Moss, Beverly Christie,

The Fifth Patient

Kathleen Sullivan, Pam Brooks
10/8/10: Bill Winslow, John Nunley, Chris Burdett, Tom
Richardson, Barry Balough

Sanger reached deeper into the envelope and pulled out a handwritten note on Dr. Connolly's letterhead.

Didn't know how to broach this in our transition meeting. Wallace Harper will be stopping by to introduce himself. Thought it was easier to let him explain. Give him the names, Pete. For the good of the hospital. Give him the names.

Sanger turned the envelope upside down. The yellow notes fell like dead leaves across his desk.

Bureau of Aging and Mortality. You've got to be kidding me.

***

The next day, Sanger planned to spend two hours in his daughter's room before heading to his office on the ninth floor. She slept most of the time, but woke long enough to see he was there, and to notice the small yellow pad in his lap.

As soon as she would awaken, he'd stand by her bedside and smile, waiting to see if she was up for good or just teasing him before falling back asleep, tangled in a fog of painkillers and antibiotics. When she slept, he would sit back down in the plaid fabric chair and review the master list of hospital patients in Wallace's manila folder.

Sanger first focused on the medical center's hospice admittance report. Northwestern Memorial Hospital had no dedicated hospice care, but it did have several rooms reserved for those who were waiting transport to Unity Hospice. These patients were goners. It was just a matter of time.

Two names came from the hospice wing. The average wait to get a bed at Unity Hospice was four days, well within Wallace's seven-day window. The next name came from the ICU. ICU patients had the most serious conditions and highest risk of complications. The staff referred to the ICU, not as the intensive care unit, but as "God's waiting room."

No one would second-guess patients punching out in the hospice rooms, but ICU was another story. ICU patients undergo constant monitoring, and the board scrutinizes any patient deaths. Still, ICU deaths were more statistically probable than any other place in the hospital. Plus, it was his first attempt at playing God, so Sanger went for the low-hanging fruit.

Three.

The medical center's ORs were the next logical place to look. Complications happen. Routine surgeries can produce nicked arteries, internal bleeding, and nasty infections. It's all in the fine print of the form every patient signs but never reads. Sanger reviewed the surgery schedule and selected a middle-aged cancer survivor who was slated for a heart valve replacement on Monday. She wasn't going to make it.

That's four.

The infamous Suzanna Eubanks, who was doing her second tour in six months for pneumonia, rounded out Sanger's starting line up. The ninety-one year old had the vocabulary of a drunken frat boy and the right hook of a champion lightweight. In March the hospital chaplain prayed over her when she was unconscious for two days. When he raised his bowed head, a plastic water cup bounced off his shoulder. Suzanna asked what he was doing at the foot of her bed and reminded him the cup wasn't going to fill itself.

Sanger was certain this stay would be her last. She'd slipped into a coma yesterday, and her vitals were weak.

Five. That's it.

By the time he finished writing Suzanna Eubanks on his own yellow post-it, his daughter was awake and looking for her breakfast. He tucked the square into a white envelope and wrote

Wallace's name on the front.

Sanger checked his watch. *Isabel's meal should be here by now.*

"Let me check on your breakfast, sweetheart. I'll be back in a sec."

***

When her door swung open, Isabel Sanger expected to see her father with a meal tray. She didn't expect to see the tall man in a gray suit and hat.

"Hello, Isabel. My name's Wallace Harper. I'm a friend of your father. I wanted to stop by and drop these off." He placed a bouquet of lilies on the overbed table. The yellow flowers sprung out of a small wicker basket. A white teddy bear with a stethoscope around its neck and a medical bag in its hand clung to the basket's handle. A silver get-well balloon bobbed over the arrangement.

"Thank you," said Isabel. "They're very pretty." She leaned forward to smell the bouquet and then pulled one of the stems from the vase. "Why don't you keep one? You could use some color."

With a smile, Wallace slipped the flower into the buttonhole on his lapel. "Better?"

"Much," said Isabel.

"How are you feeling?"

"Not too bad. Really sleepy. I want to go home, but my dad says I have to be on this stuff for a few days." Isabel pointed to the wrinkled IV bag hanging next to her bed.

"I'm sure you'll be right as rain in a few days." Wallace turned toward the door. "Please tell your father I stopped by. And get well soon."

"You just missed him. He's trying to find my breakfast."

"I passed the breakfast cart down the hall. Looks like pancakes." Wallace smiled again. He had one foot in the hall when Isabel called for him.

"Don't forget your envelope."

"My what?" said Wallace.

"Your envelope. There, on the chair. Your name's on it. Unless he's leaving it for another Wallace Harper."

Wallace eyed the envelope for a moment before snatching it from the chair and tucking it in his inside jacket pocket. "Thank you, Isabel. You've been a big help."

"Thanks for the flowers," she said to the closing door.

***

Wallace followed Sanger into the Chicago Avenue red line stop. Sanger shook the rain off his umbrella and waited for the L to Fullerton Street. A young girl bumped into him as she moved her arms like train wheels chugging between the waiting passengers on the platform. Her mother apologized, and with a grin, yanked her daughter closer. The girl tooted her imaginary whistle as Wallace placed a hand on Sanger's shoulder.

"I figured you'd be staying at the hospital," said Wallace. "With your daughter."

"I've been there for two days straight. My wife's there tonight. I'm going home to get some sleep. Got to have a clear head tomorrow."

Wallace fumbled in his pocket, pulling out the yellow square. "About your list," he said. "You only gave me four patients."

"I gave you five."

"You gave me five names, but only four patients."

Sanger plucked it from his hand. "What are you talking about?"

"See here," Wallace pointed. "Suzanna Eubanks. She was discharged this afternoon. I hear she had a miraculous recovery. She's no longer in play."

"Bullshit. You said five patients. She was a patient when I wrote the list."

"Doesn't matter. She left the hospital. I can't take her."

"I'll give you another name tomorrow."

"I'm sorry. I told you, paperwork is due upstairs by eight o'clock." He pulled up the sleeve on his gray overcoat and tapped his watch. "No exceptions."

"What do you expect me to do?"

"I expect you to get it right next time, Dr. Sanger." Wallace took the note back, pulled the small green pencil from behind his ear and crossed Suzanna Eubanks' name from the list.

The concrete platform shook as the red L train rumbled around the corner and into the station. When it stopped, the metal and glass doors shuddered open behind Sanger.

The young girl and her mother had disappeared into the gathering crowd, which surged forward into the waiting train car. A flash of faces and elbows pushed Sanger onto the train, and the closing doors kept him there.

"Don't worry," Wallace shouted over the hissing train. "I added the fifth name for you." The train's air brakes popped and it lurched forward.

Wallace pulled the yellow lily from his lapel and twirled it between his fingers. Watching the train disappear into the night, he brought the flower to his nose before tossing it to the tracks.

About the author: Trace Conger is an award-winning author in the crime, thriller and suspense genres. His Mr. Finn series follows disgraced private investigator Finn Harding as he straddles the fine line between investigator and criminal. Conger lives in Cincinnati with his wonderfully supportive family. Find out more about him and his work at www.traceconger.com

Sleep Driving

By Angela Lambert

Kelvin pressed against the wound as blood seeped around his hands. That's me, Kelvin. I could almost see myself doing this as if it was some kind of out-of-body experience. Adrenaline rushed through my veins and my mind raced in frantic directions. Her need to show me, beckoned her dying heart to pump the last of her blood, through her otherwise still remains. It happened again. There was a wrong that needed to be made right. But by the time I'd reached her, she was purpled with proof and almost gone. In her final moments, she forcibly fed me every turn in the road and frightful emotion until I lapped-in the savage mordant details.

****

When I opened my eyes, my legs quivered as I looked over her now lifeless body. Her auburn locks of hair blended into the sandy soil as the earth spattered vomit onto her porcelain flesh. Her right hand was broken and distorted, yet her muddied fingers clutched a flower stem. I leaned over and gently removed the flower. A mixture of tears and rain wetted my face. My forehead wrinkled with not only dread but also worry. How had fate allowed her delicate body to be mangled, her tender face to drown in this gruesome situation?

It hadn't happen for a while, until this morning. I woke up just before daybreak in a strange place with a death at my hands. I can't remember if I took a Zolpidem before hitting the pillow, or should I say pavement, last night. Maybe I took a whole one this time, instead of half—I'm just not sure. The older I get, the less I'm able to recall the details. After all, the pill is small, tiny even.

I don't tell the doctors it happens anymore because they don't believe me anyway. If I said I had pain, then I would easily get a script for hydrocodone, at the very least. If I said my pain wasn't controlled, even after taking five tablets a day, I would easily get an Opana or Oxycontin script. Tell the doctors I lose hours at times, during the night, and all I get is a prescription for more sleeping pills, at a higher dose, and a return appointment for next month. I've tried everything, from hiding the keys to leaving the van out of gas, but nothing works. I always find a way to get to them.

***

I stepped through the tall corn and onto the edge of the field, leaving her remains for someone else to find.

"She was almost in the clear. I can see the station from here," I whispered, under my breath. "Here we go again."

I left the cornfield, with muddied boots, and approached the van. The rain removed each of my footprints like an eraser wiping away troubling chalkboard math equations. I saw Cyrus' wide-eyes peering toward me through the rain-covered windshield. I don't know why this sort of thing scares him. It has been going on for years. He should have climbed in the back to sleep. At least one of us would have gotten some rest. Cyrus has lived most of his life in Point Pleasant, amid compact spaces of the cold frame back home. Though it seems we only get a chance to visit during unfortunate circumstances.

Before reaching for the door handle, I pulled my handkerchief from my hip pocket and wiped the remainder of her blood from my hand and gently placed the flower between the bloodstained folds of the tender fabric. Again, the pouring rain did a pretty good job of showering away most of the mess, on its own. The van door squeaked open to permit entrance and I took my seat behind the wheel.

"What this time?" Cyrus said.

"Her name was Violet. I knew how she was tortured and how her body got all the way out here. Hopefully, I'll be able to scratch down the answer to who killed her so she can rest in peace."

***

The train station wasn't busy, but then again times have changed. Few cars, less than four, sprinkled the parking lot.

The means, by which we had traveled through the night, from West Virginia through Ohio only to land in Michigan, remained a mystery.

"Hey, could you pull the map from the glove box and get us home, Cyrus? You know I cannot tell heads nor tales about those things."

"Already thinking the same thing."

"The train depot says, Pontiac, MI."

"I'm already on it." Cyrus wiggled in his seat and wiped a circular design in the passenger door glass as he looked away from me, after briefly studying the map. "And another thing that I was thinking is that we haven't been together like this for a long time..."

"I know. Don't get used to it. I can't imagine either of us have missed this tour of duty. By the way things looked, she really needed us to find her tonight."

***

That sickening feeling was settling in my stomach. I could feel my hands on her blood again. You know the smell, that of rotting flesh

27

being fed on by maggots or it could be the aroma of the molded vinyl seats in the van renewed by the rainy night. It was definitely one of those noisome pockets of memory spurring the nausea. Piecing the night together would be time consuming and a task I was hoping never to have to face again.

"First things first. How about breakfast?" Kelvin said. "I'm starving and I bet Michigan has a Waffle House on the horizon somewhere."

"Now you're cooking!"

"What'll it be? Scattered, smothered, or covered taters this time?"

"Smothered and chunked, for sure," Cyrus said.

"Scattered for me, this time. I'll think better with some food on my stomach."

"Then can we talk about her? Huh? Then can we—on the drive back home?"

"Sure. In the meantime, keep your eyes peeled for a Waffle House sign."

"Hello! My name is Amelia." The waitress smacked her gum around her mouth like a pinball in a busy machine. She was easily too young to be expecting but nonetheless the service was pleasant. "What will it be for ya on this early, August, morning?"

Cyrus gave his order and looked at me.

"Two eggs, over easy, scattered with hash browns, and a coffee that will stand up without a cup. Also, one scrambled egg, smothered and chunked hash browns, and a tall glass of chocolate milk. Oh, and ketchup," I said.

"Anything else I can bring your way, just let me know. I'll be right back with the drinks."

"I'm headed to the bathroom," I said. "Need to wash my hands and splash some water on my face."

"Sure. Then, when you get back, we can talk about her."

"Not here. Let's wait until we get back in the van."

"Sure."

***

Breakfast was served. Forks and knives clambered as the eggs and scattered hash browns were scraped up and shoveled in. I instinctively reached for my handkerchief, glanced at Cyrus to see if he had noticed, and pulled the paper napkin to my face instead. After the second cup of coffee was poured, I emptied it in four gulps. "Ahhh."

"Can I take your plates, sir?"

"You sure can," I said.

"Is there something wrong with the other order? I would be glad to fix it for you, if there is."

"No—just eyes bigger than appetite."

"Sure thing. I'll be right back with the check."

"Why did you order all that food if you weren't planning on eating it?"

"I've lost my appetite," I said.

"It's the girl—"

"Hush, until we get out of here."

"Sure thing."

"Here's your check, sir. You have a great day and come back."

I touched the waitress on her elbow. "If you don't mind me asking...Amelia, right?"

"Yes, that's my name."

"What's your favorite flower, Amelia?"

"Well...I guess it would be a daisy. Why do you ask?"

"Hmmm...a daisy. That's a late spring bloomer. Good choice, Amelia."

Amelia blushed at the added attention. "Why, thank you."

"Here's a fifty, Amelia-that-loves-daisies. Keep the change." As I gestured towards her baby bump, I said, "It looks like you will be needing it in more ways than one.""Thank you! I sure will put it to good use. You stop by again, now."

I could not help but notice Amelia as she returned a questionable smile, a smack of gum to her left molar, and one last curious glance over her right shoulder.

"Oh, we will."

***

The van, barely visible through the veil of pouring rain, seemed farther from the door than Kelvin remembered. With each boot step echoing a thud across the pavement, reaching the van quickly became an obstacle. Just when the despair of not finding the keys was about to take over, I found them in my right, front pant pocket under the crumpled breakfast receipt.

"Who chose this parking place?" I said. "It'll take the better part of the drive home to dry off."

"It don't matter. We got nothing better to do but talk about her for hours, anyway."

After sliding the key in the ignition and twisting it with a forward turn, I started the engine. The van exhaled a puff of smoke out of the exhaust pipe.

"True," I said. "Right or left—which way out of here?"

***

I was never so glad to see Point Pleasant. As a result of the road trip, I would get a late start to my workday at the nursery. Getting the summer beds cleaned up and ready for winter was not an easy chore. When my parents were living, it made the work much more tolerable. With Dad helping, the workload was cut in half. After my parents passed, it seemed the right thing to do in continuing the family business, like it or not. Cyrus wasn't much for digging in the dirt, therefore offered moral support more than anything else.

Sleep Driving

With the heavy burden of another sleep driving incident weighing on me, and with the details of her death left unclear, the season changed. The writing hadn't chosen to reveal yet. It will. It always does. The details, ever so vivid, ever so exact.

***

The nursery remained steady until after the holidays. With January came a little free time. Discussing, in great detail, everything from expected precipitation to dormant vegetation, I put my pen to paper and outlined my monthly gardening column for February. Local readers looked forward to my helpful gardening hints and guidance, at the start of each month. My unique writing gift, or burden, in some cases, didn't stop there.

It was time.

I walked to the old desk in the corner of the kitchen porch. Corners are good places for things left to gather dust and other things that are not wanted. The drawer scraped with apprehension but allowed me in. I shuffled through and pulled a pad of paper, edges bent and burned due to age, from the second drawer down on the left. The drawer returned a scrape as an obvious sigh of closure. I pulled the wooden knob, on the shallow center drawer, dug in, and returned with a number two lead pencil, tattooed with floral buds. There were only three, half-spent, left rolling around in the drawer, like a cat in heat, as if asking to be used. I moved my fingers, with gentleness, and shoved the drawer shut.

I took the tools and walked to the north corner of the greenhouse. Smells of dirt and sounds of flapping plastic filled the air, equally familiar. I had a comfortable corner in mind and the company of Cyrus, once again. Looking to Cyrus with a hollow gaze, I started to scratch the pencil to paper.

***

My name was Violet Elizabeth Vanhorn. I bloomed in late July and named my blossom Iris Elizabeth Vanhorn. She was beautiful. They came to my house, in the night, so I ran. I wanted to distract them away from her and my mother. I thought that if I could lure them away, it would save my girls. I only pray that it worked.

***

They chased me from the house, across the fence, through the garden, then into the cornfield. I ran as fast as I could. There were too many of them—four, at least. I recognized two of them, the Tobin boys, from out Stingy Creek Road. Why do people do the things they do, Kelvin? I tripped, fell, and ripped my dress. I stood back up, but it got stuck under my foot or something. I felt one grab my ankle. It burned so he must have taken some hide. I got up again and ran farther—I had to get as far from the house as I could. This time I ran directly into one of them. I looked right into Matt Tobin's eyes, but he wasn't there. Instead, an animal was there with eyes as black as coal. I guess he headed me off while the others chased from behind. One grabbed me by my hair. I had my mother's thick, red hair but that was a hindrance because it gave them more to grasp hold of. I know it came out because I felt the yank and burn with each handful. I struggled but they were stronger. It hurt, Kelvin, and bad. But in order to save my girls, I would endure it again. When my bones broke and pulled from me, that's when I couldn't feel the pain anymore. I nearly made it to the train station, but the corn was thick and tall, sharp and slick. At the end, I could see you driving toward me, Kelvin. I knew you would get here. I kept the flower so you would find me. I must have yanked it from the grass, without noticing as I ran to save their lives. I met you once, in a coffee shop in Lewisburg. You asked me what my favorite flower was. I told you violet, of course because it was my name. The flowers are your beacons, Kelvin. They are your glowing gift. Would you see that my girls are safe? Would you please, Kelvin? As for those boys, you know what to do about them.

***

As I pressed harder, through the sobbing and quivering scribbles, I revealed the fateful end of Violet's life. The destination of my sleep driving to Pontiac, Michigan was on account of Violet Elizabeth Vanhorn.

***

The greenhouse was quiet and cold and wind blew just enough to toss the hint of her presence against the walls as I hunched over the outcome. The plastic then cracked against the air and released a silence—she was gone.

"I'm sorry for her, Kelvin," Cyrus said.

"Me too. Why couldn't we have driven faster and gotten there just a little sooner? She was nearly at the train station."

"She was, but we weren't, Kelvin. Just like all the other times, we never get there quickly enough."

***

The night fell deeper and the air colder. If it were not for the heat lamps on the forced beds, I would have frozen that night, in the greenhouse.

Cyrus tried to arouse me several times. "Kelvin, wake up! Wake up, Kelvin, you gotta get in the house. Kelvin, come on, Kelvin, wake up!"

***

The early morning sun added more heat to the greenhouse and the timers buzzed when the heat lamps kicked off for the day. My body was worse for wear and moving in slow motion. The fate of a twisted night had left me stiffened but with closure. "Cyrus, are you there?"

"I'm here."

"Get ready. We have a road trip to make today."

"I have been expecting it and I'm ready when you are."

"Can you map us a route to Pontiac, Michigan? I slept on the way there during our first trip."

"Sure can."

***

The drive didn't seem as long as the one last August. At least the snow held off and the roads remained relatively clear. Some folks were even outside removing holiday decorations from the eaves—surely the want of their wives.

With the train station close, Cyrus stuffed the crumpled map back into the glove box. "Hey, look what I found, a new box of pencils! Tattooed with floral buds just like the ones in your desk."

My gaze swept across Cyrus, with unresponsive emotion.

PLUNK! The right, front tire hit a pothole and then the right, rear tire brushed its edge.

"Never you mind them right now, Kelvin. I will stuff them back in. You know we could stop at the Waffle House again."

"I suppose we could."

"Her name was Amelia, remember?"

"Daisies are much prettier than they smell." I said. "Don't you agree?"

"For sure."

***

Sleep Driving

We arrived at the train station and parked the van just before darkness fell. We peered over toward the now cleared cornfield. Tattered orange tape snapped in the wind, while wrapped and tied to four posts marking the gruesome discovery of her remains.

I watched a woman carry a small child from the edge of the cornfield to the train station parking lot. The woman carefully placed the little one in a car seat and glanced one last time to the cornfield. She brushed her glove under tear-stained eyes, before getting into the car to drive away.

I waited until just before the 9:00 P.M. train was to pass. I stepped out of van with Cyrus alongside. I reached into my left jacket pocket and pulled the tattered violet from the bloodstained handkerchief.

"Rest, Violet Elizabeth Vanhorn, your girls are together and safe tonight."

The air filled with the resounding whistle blow of the train passing through the station as I handed Cyrus the violet. Watching the train disappear into the night, he brought the flower to his nose before tossing it to the tracks.

About the author: Angela Lambert is a writer, photographer, and illustrator. She spent twenty years as a practicing pharmacist and now devotes her time to the creative arts of fictional mysteries and storytelling photography. Her artwork has been featured in myriad galleries both nationally and internationally. She is a Getty Artist and a Tamarack Artisan. Angela's writing, richly steeped in lore and influenced by her upbringing in rural Appalachia, brings mystery and thrilling adventures to print. She now resides in coastal New Jersey.

The Fall of Sleep

by J. Mace

Kelvin pressed against the wound as blood seeped around his hands. "This is gonna take a bit more than wishful thinking, son."

"It's okay, dad. We gotta get this thing finished. Last one there's a big dope."

"Doesn't matter, this ain't gonna stop bleeding 'less we wrap it. And stop with that word. Your mother hates it."

"Just hurry. It's gonna be dark soon, and I hate to walk down there when..."

"Get in there and you won't have to worry 'bout it."

The boy hopped onto the porch and left a red handprint on the aluminum door. A trail of red drops was splattered on the bright green porch.

"I just painted that." Kelvin sighed. "Don't get that on the carpet either. You'll get us both whipped."

Teri's frantic voice drifted through the screen door just as Kelvin's foot touched the first step. He avoided the half-butchered pumpkin and his wife's best kitchen knife, and followed his ten-year old son inside.

***

Kelvin couldn't stop thinking about Dale. Four years. His hands were crossed with smooth, shiny scars. Tic marks for each year since he'd been doing this for his son.

"Damn." His hands shook. The knife clanged to the cement. Drops of blood fell to the porch and splattered on the faded green paint. "Think I'd be gettin' better at this."

The sun, fat and orange, squatted on the horizon line, and the breeze, which had been blowing warm from the south all day, suddenly felt ten degrees cooler. Dark clouds swirled and clung to the tops of the northern tree line.

Cold tonight. Frost maybe.

He stuck the injured finger in his mouth. The wound burned, and when he spit a mouthful of coppery blood into the grass, he realized how deep he'd cut it.

"Gonna take a bit more than wishful thinking."

His knees crackled, and a cool ache spread across the back of his legs. He stepped over the half finished jack-o-lantern, avoided Teri's rusted knife, and opened the screen door.

"Damn." He said. His palm print, shiny and red, glowed on the white door. "This is your fault." He told the butchered pumpkin. "But you're not gettin' off easy. I'm still taking you."

He went inside.

Last one there's a big dope.

***

"Looks good, son," Kelvin said. "Always does."

"Good's not enough. Good won't win anything."

"It's about the competition, I'd say. More than anything."

"I know." Dale put the jack-o-lantern back on the porch and stepped back. The fat bandage on his finger was stained orange. It was perhaps fifteen minutes before the mountain swallowed the top of the sun, but already, the pumpkin's shadow stretched the length of the porch and spilled onto the dying grass. "Is it scary enough?"

"I'd say so, yes." Kelvin shivered. His stomach ached for the boy. In what nightmare, from what ink-black hallway had *this* face been dragged from? He shivered again. Freakish wasn't the right word for it. Freakish implied at least some human characteristics. This butchered expression had nothing to do with anything human. This monstrosity was by far the worst Kelvin had ever seen.

«Wait," Dale said. The knife was in his hand, his shoulders worked. His back blocked Kelvin's view. He watched a shadow crawl up his son's leg.

"Better get a move on." A tingling at the base of his neck. The boy had forgotten about the dark. "We still gotta carry it down there."

"Got it." Dale said and stepped back to reveal his work.

And Kelvin saw that he had been wrong.

Now.

Now it was the worst he'd ever seen.

***

Kelvin's finger had finally stopped bleeding. Teri had always teased him about how when he'd start a project, she'd start collecting bandages and ointment because it was only a matter of time. Dale had always been that way, too. *Like father...*

He held the pumpkin up and studied it. Besides one crooked eyehole, his creation was nothing special. It wouldn't even come close to Dale's. The jagged mouth and nose too crudely carved. The work of a child. Or an old man's weak fingers. An old man whose knuckles were calcified knobs the size of grapes. An old man whose soft, alcoholic tremors drew pained sighs from strangers.

"Not scary at all," he said and chuckled. "Maybe with a little light."

Two minutes of struggling found him lighting the candle

jammed into the pumpkin's sloppy insides. He stepped back until his heels just touched the sunset's closing shadow.

Kelvin laughed. Louder than he should have. His neighbors already seemed unsure of themselves around him.

"This thing wouldn't scare a baby," he said. "Dale would love it." His blood went cold at saying it. "Dale's *gonna* love it. He's *gonna* love it."

Things did feel different this year. Better somehow.

He turned the jack-o-lantern toward the darkness and asked, "You like it?"

*****

The Grey Mountain Fall Festival was the annual celebration of everything autumn. It had though, through the years, become more than an end of summer celebration. For some reason no one alive could remember, the festival had been pushed to the final week of October and it took on a mostly Halloween theme. Besides the candy corn-themed cooking contest and the maple leaf fun run, the most popular event by far was the Halloween Jack-O-Lantern Contest.

The train station, near the center of town, served as the contest's home—a five-foot high retaining wall, and a three-foot tall wooden stage placed in front of it, held the entries aloft. The annual contest saw hundreds of pumpkins filling the red and yellow ribbon-wrapped walls.

The entries ran the gamut. From a portrait of the town's mayor to Frankenstein's monster. Each one lovingly placed and illuminated each night. The entire week before judging, the Rotary Club oversaw the nightly lighting of the candles. Usually, the council of judges had just enough time to make their decisions before the sun and the fruit flies softened the works of art to mush.

It was here that two-year-old Dale had been frightened to tears before his eyes dried to amazement and wonder.

The Fall of Sleep

They're all staring at me, Daddy.

Thinking about it now though, which Kelvin admitted he'd done an awful lot of since Dale had gone, it seemed that might have been when his son's troubles began. Sort of like a switch had been flipped that turned on some darkness inside him. A door opened that had splashed black paint on the boy's insides. All the terrible things that poured in with it. Dark thoughts. Dark cravings.

"I wanna do it. I wanna make one," the little boy had said, his cheeks still red and lined with shiny trails. And he had every year since. Despite his mother's protests.

Kelvin wished he'd listened to Teri.

His son's creations had become more disturbing each year.

***

During the winter of Dale's thirteenth year on earth, shadows darker than fever burned nightmares, swept in and opened death's door. A cold wind, stinking of cancer and chemicals, and radiation-burned insides, picked Teri up, and not so gently, carried her inside.

***

"She woulda loved it," Kelvin said. It was the first October since Teri left them. A tightness had settled in his guts since the funeral and had refused to leave.

"I don't know." Dale turned the face back and forth on the porch. "I can hear her saying, 'Dale Thomas, that is the most hideous thing I've ever seen.'"

Kelvin smiled. "Well, I suppose that's what you wanted to hear, wasn't it?"

"Yeah," Dale said. A large grin spread across his face for a moment before his gaze dropped as he picked at one corner of the pumpkin's mouth. "She loved the festival, didn't she? I could tell she was just acting like she didn't."

Kelvin nodded. *What she didn't like was what you're doing right now. Never did.* "Her favorite time of year. The fall of sleep, she used to call it, and I always liked the way she said that, like it was a poem."

Dale ran his finger around inside the pumpkin's mouth. Kelvin couldn't understand how the boy made such realistic teeth with just a knife and a paper clip. His son wiped his finger on his jeans. The shadows had begun to creep closer to the house, closer to both of them. Soft fog blew from their mouths with each breath. "Why'd it have to happen like it did? Why'd it happen so fast?"

"I don't know, son. Things sometimes work out that way."

Dale turned, staring out into the darkness. He seemed to shudder. "I didn't get to really say goodbye to her, you know. Everybody was talking about her being sick, and trying to figure out how to deal with it, and all of a sudden she was gone." His hand disappeared into his jacket pocket, and retrieved a dried yellow flower.

"A marigold. Her favorite. From the funeral." He poked the cut stem carefully into the pumpkin's cap. "It'll be good luck. You think?"

Kelvin nodded. He started to speak, but the words stuck in his throat. The tightness in his gut spread lower. He walked over to his son and embraced him.

There was nothing else to say.

***

Two years later, there was still nothing else to say.

"I don't care if I win."

"Why do it then?"

"I don't...I don't know. We've always done it."

"That doesn't seem like much of a reason to—"

"I'm afraid not to." He smiled, but it was edged with darkness.

"Afraid?"

"Yeah. I guess it's silly, but..." Dale put the knife on the porch.

"It feels like they'll finally catch me if I don't do this." He held the glowing face. Shadows from the carvings edged forward, slipped back, from the wobbling flame. The glow reflected in Dale's eyes. Pinpoints of light shined from their centers. Kelvin shivered.

Dale stared into the darkness. His head tilted from side to side. The candlelight fought the approaching dark.

Kelvin slowed his breathing. He couldn't hear anything but the wind. The sensation that he was being watched settled over him like a blanket. "Son?"

The boy's eyes had clouded over, the reflection of candle flame extinguished. "Yeah Dad?"

"It's the nightmares again?"

"Yeah."

"How often?"

"Every night."

"Son."

"During the day, too."

"They the same?"

"Yeah. Being chased." The corners of his mouth turned down. "Used to be when I'd wake up, especially if it was still dark, I'd feel like I was still in it. Like they were still after me. Soon as the light started coming in my window, I'd feel a little better. But now though..." He shook his head.

An overwhelming sadness gripped Kelvin. Dale used to get himself worked up when he was little, staying up late and watching scary movies. But any nightmares from them seemed to dissipate after a few days. At least until he watched another one. Teri had been surprisingly lenient about it. Her rule was that if he scared himself, he'd just have to deal with it. No sleeping with Mommy and Daddy.

You want scary? Fine. But suffer alone.

When Teri passed, Dale started waking most nights. Once, when Kelvin had been awakened by Dale's terrible screams, he'd staggered into the room, flipped the light switch, and found Dale wound in his blankets, eyes closed, mouth twisted in agony. Pushing himself against the headboard, feet kicking, hands clawing.

"Something was chasing me." His t-shirt dark with sweat, his hair soaked.

"What was it?"

"I don't know. I'm not sure. I never see the faces."

"I'm here. It's okay now."

It wasn't. The nightmares had intensified. Months had passed before the screams had stopped, and Dale had quit answering questions about it. Kelvin had decided it was best to let his son decide when to talk.

But Teri had been gone for nearly three years. Why the fear again?

A pang of guilt gnawed at Kelvin. The idea that his son had been suffering quietly hit him hard.

Dale hefted the jack-o-lantern and stood on the porch. He turned the glowing face to Kelvin. To the darkness. The boy stared past him, and for a moment, the air pressed close to Kelvin's back— hot air, wet as if from tortured lungs, drifted across his neck. He shivered despite its heat, and turned to face the darkness.

"You like it?" Dale asked.

When Kelvin turned to answer him, the boy wasn't looking at him, he was staring hard into the black. Defiant. Same as the jack-o'-lantern.

Years later, quicker than seemed possible, Kelvin found himself wishing the boy still needed him.

He'd told Kelvin the terrible news that October as they walked the dirt path to the train station. Dale had finished the carving early, when the sun was still bright in the sky. Most of the leaves had fallen, but some wind kept the path clear. The wagon's squeaky wheel was the only sound until Dale broke the silence.

"I'm going, Dad."

"Son." His heart swelled with fear and pride. His legs were stiff and useless.

"I've made up my mind."

"You're too damn young."

"I'm twenty."

"Not for six months yet." Despite the sun, cold seemed to rise from the ground and slip beneath his clothes. "You're a teenager."

Dale shook his head and walked. The wagon's wheel squeaked, and Kelvin was aware of how dull the paint was. "I'm plenty old."

Kelvin's mind raced. His sweatshirt was damp now, heavy as a lead vest. "You listen to me. Get the idea out of your head." He grabbed Dale's shoulder. "You can go to school, or get a job. That's what you need. I'll help you."

"I'm not cut out for school. Besides, I can't stay here."

"Why? The dreams?"

"They're more than dreams, Dad."

"Your mother would—"

"She's dead. Six years dead." His face softened, and he touched Kelvin's arm. "I just need to get away. You know?"

Kelvin sighed. He did know. He'd felt like hopping in the car and driving away as soon as the funeral ended, but something kept him here. Like leaving was somehow disrespectful to Teri's memory. He nodded. His son was dealing with more than he ever had.

"I think Mom would want me to get out of here."

Kelvin nodded again. *But not like this.* "Let's get this to the station. See if you can finally win one."

Dale smiled at him. A broad, toothy grin that reminded Kelvin so much of Teri's. It was the last time Kelvin would remember seeing it.

***

When he came home the first time, Dale's face was blank. His eyes dark. He had stepped from the train, his uniform pressed and stiff, and offered Kelvin his hand. Kelvin had eased into talking about it. He'd read all the pamphlets. Dale had refused him. A nod. A shake of the head. So he didn't press. In the short time he was home, Dale stayed up late. He barely ate. "I've seen them all." He said one evening as the sun dipped lower and their empty bottles piled higher. "Every single one of them."

"Seen what, son?" Inside Kelvin's head, the alcoholic buzz sparked and went out. His warm insides went cold.

"The pumpkins." His expression didn't change. "I've seen all of their faces out there."

Forty-eight hours later, the train took him away again. Took him back.

Kelvin dragged the wagon. The moon was out, full and bright behind the thin and finger-like apple tree branches. Behind him, the shadows ran across the path. Changing places. Whispering. He tried to ignore them. For a moment, he wanted to light the pumpkin and turn it towards them, but he thought better.

He'd always chased them away, but not this year. This year he wanted them with him. Maybe they'd find his son. After all, hadn't they chased him away?

The jack-o-lantern, could never top Dale's. No matter how many times he tried. The almost human faces, twisted in agony, enduring unseen tortures. Although, he supposed, Dale had an advantage. Tears welled up and spilled onto his cheeks.

He stopped the wagon.

Startled shadows wrapped themselves around tree trunks. Hid behind rolling, dried apple leaves. Shot up to cover the moon.

Kelvin unfolded his fist and placed the dried marigold on the pumpkin, and headed to the station.

***

It had been late. And Kelvin was dreaming of Dale as a boy. Dreaming while he waited for Dale's second return.

His pounding nails into ten-year-old Dale's tree house had transformed into a knocking on his front door. He shook himself awake, pulled himself up from his recliner, and stumbled to answer it.

Two men, spines arrow straight, official in their dress and their jutting chins. A letter. Soft words of encouragement. After they'd driven away, Kelvin became more and more unsure if they had been there at all. The next morning there were still tire tracks on his driveway. And there was the letter. Sitting on the kitchen table where he guessed he had tossed it.

The words seemed jumbled. Nonsensical.

Missing.
Whereabouts unknown.
Kelvin was sure of it now. A joke.
Dale was coming home.
Home by Halloween.

***

Each year became the next became the next. The shadows followed Kelvin along the path to the train station. That was fine with him as long as they left Dale alone. Each year they drew closer. Starved of his son.

***

He pulled the wagon onto the concrete platform as the train whistle sounded in the distance. The station was nearly empty. A worker, glowing beneath a fluorescent light, swept cigarette butts and twisted leaves into a dustpan. A man, bundled in a dark coat, was hunched over on a bench.

Kelvin rolled the wagon close to the pumpkin display. And

gasped. His heart drummed a staccato rhythm. He couldn't breathe. The display was full, as full as he could remember, the candles bright. Faces pushed out and projected onto the gathering fog. His blood froze. His breath came in ragged bursts. He staggered back.

The jack-o-lanterns, their malformed faces, wobbled and shook in the swirling fog. A huge toothless mouth swallowing whole, smiling eyes. Another face, hungry teeth bared, pushed through another's smooth head, shredding and chewing from the inside. Misshapen, bulging eyes stared blindly. Candlelight bursting through as fiery roasted pumpkin seeds. A nightmare of cannibal feasts. A battlefield of agony. And Dale in the fog. His mouth pushed into a thin line. His eyes squeezed shut. His hands pressed hard to his ears.

The train whistle was louder now.

Kelvin remembered his words. *I've seen them all.*

His legs weakened, and he nearly fell, but was propped up by the shadows. Pushing him up and up. The jack-o-lanterns had driven him to the edge of the tracks. The ground rumbled. The air vibrated. The train so close it shook his teeth. It rolled to a stop without Dale, as it always would.

Kelvin found the wagon tipped over and emptied. Beside it, the dried flower was crushed, flattened by his wild retreat. His creation shattered amid the gnarled, grinning faces. His *creations.* Forever lost in the nightmare. And he understood that it was good that Dale was gone. Good for Dale.

Watching the train disappear into the night, he brought the flower to his nose before tossing it to the tracks.

About the author: J. Mace picked up his typewriter at the ripe old age of thirty-eight. These many years later, when he's not at his day job, he finds time to write unsettling stories based on his unreasonable fears of serial killers and unlocked doors. More insight into J's tortured mind can be found on his twitter feed @readJmace, and on his website at www.readjmace.wordpress.com.

Got To Keep Moving

by Katherine Sanger

Kelvin pressed against the wound as blood seeped around his hands. The pain and the sticky-wet feeling of his jeans made him realize he was in more trouble than he'd thought. And the evening had started out so well.

He was home from college on Thanksgiving break, and Celia and he had a date at the only nice restaurant in town. It had tablecloths (even if they were made of plastic and not actual cloth), a hostess (even if she did wear overalls with her white frilly shirt poking through the straps), and a dance floor, even though it was kept dark because the parquet had long ago given up the ghost and lost its attachment to the concrete slab underneath.

Celia ordered dessert to split, meaning he'd sit there and watch her eat, being more an excuse than an actual partner.

"Look, you're a really nice guy and all," she said. "But, well, it's not you. It's me. No, it's not even me. It's my father."

"What are you saying?" Kelvin went with the old-fashioned delaying tactic. He'd like the relationship to at least survive until he paid for the meal. It only seemed right that he should get a full date out of it if he was the one ponying up the money.

Celia sighed and futzed with her hair, pulling her blonde curly mane from the scrunchy, then taming it back again.

"What I'm saying is…it's over. Between us. It's just, see, my daddy promised me a T-Bird if I broke up with you. And, here's the thing…" She squared her shoulders and seemed to find center. "My father is kind of like a demon. You know, from hell?"

Kelvin leaned back in his chair, putting as much distance as possible between him and his now ex, probably always crazy, girlfriend. But as crazy as her statement sounded, things started to fall in place. The way her house was always so hot. The room that had its hurricane shutter permanently affixed. The weird screams and sulphur-like smell that hung in the air around her house that she said was swamp gas. He'd never heard of swamp gas making noise before, but he'd accepted her explanation because she was cute and perky and put out.

The expression on his face must have been doing the talking for him because she spoke again.

"Yeah, weird, right? Anyway, he said he'd take away my beauty and my youth and my eternal life and blah blah blah. Plus, the T-Bird is a convertible. But you've been a really sweet guy all this time, so I should probably warn you that he's sending a hellhound after you. You might want to start running. Not that it'll do any good. It never does any good. Not even for Ted." She sniffed.

Ted. Kelvin remembered Ted. He'd been the long-distance track star, and he had dated Celia before Kelvin had. And then he'd disappeared. Everyone thought he'd just run away when Celia dumped him. Celia seemed to have a lot of boyfriends who disappeared once she broke up with them. Kelvin hadn't heeded that warning, though. He thought he would be different. Of course, he also hadn't thought that demons would be involved.

"Um, Kelvin? You might want to get a head start. After you pay the check." And she smiled that smile. The one that, in the past, always made him give in to her. It still worked. But the minute he tossed the cash on the table, he was out the door, straining to hear baying or howling or any noises that might signal that a hellhound was hunting or had found him. He thought he heard panting, but that might have been his own breath.

He started for home, but stopped. Celia's dad knew where he lived. It would be easy to have the hellhounds there waiting for him. Where else could he go? Run back to college? That was one hell of a long run, and he couldn't even do a 5k.

There was a growl behind him. He tripped, stumbled, and hit the ground. Something sharp stabbed through his jeans and into his leg. He felt the wetness immediately and knew he was bleeding, but the fear of what was after him was greater than the fear of bleeding, he got back up and started running again.

Celia had driven them to dinner, so he was stuck on foot, and he wasn't as fast as Ted. Or as nimble. Which is why, as he looked over his shoulder, he ran into Brianna.

"Jesus Christ!" he said. "I thought I was dead!"

Brianna nodded. "We all feel that way some days."

"No, I meant literally...I mean—" He noticed the glint of keys in her hand. "Can I get a ride?"

"Um, sure. I guess. I mean, where are you going?" She twirled the keys.

"Somewhere else."

She nodded again. "Yeah, I've—"

"Felt that way, too," he finished for her. "Let's go."

She frowned, but shrugged. "C'mon." And she led him to her hearse.

He stared at the car. A bad omen for him? But he could feel the blood still seeping through his jeans, around his hands, and the sticky-wet feeling made him realize he was in trouble. His shins had spikes in them from the short run he'd done, and his chest pounded. So he climbed into Brianna's car.

"Brianna. You're...different."

She laughed. "That's a way to put it." She fired up the car.

"I have a problem. And maybe you're different enough to help me."

"What's the problem?"

"Well, you know my ex-girlfriend?"

He could see Brianna's eyebrows go up in the glare of the oncoming headlights.

"Ex?"

"Yeah, ex. Celia dumped me tonight because her demon father decided he didn't like me, and now he's sent a hellhound after me. And I ripped my jeans, and I'm bleeding like a sieve."

Brianna was silent. He regretted spilling it all out. Was she driving them to the closest ER to turn him in for observation? To the police station? To his parents?

"Sieves don't bleed. Let me look." She leaned over and pulled at the rip in his jeans. Poked at the gash that was still oozing blood. "I can fix you up. And I know someplace that might have a book that could help you out. We really need to get you away from people. Celia had two boyfriends mauled to death by pit bulls already. Don't you remember? Back in high school? One was in the middle of the food court. Took forever to get the stain out."

Everything began to spin and went dark.

He woke up with Brianna leaning over him, stitching his leg, the jean material around the wound cut away.

"Ouch!" He jerked, noticed that made it hurt worse, and then realized how woozy he felt.

"Don't move," she said. "I'm almost done."

"Sorry, I just, um. I think it must be from blood loss."

"Uh-huh." She kept stitching, the sharp pains from the needle poking at him, making him think. Brianna had always been the Ducky of his life. She was always around, always interested, always willing to do things for him. And he'd always used her. He'd ignored her, gotten her to help with his homework—or do it, whenever possible. And now he'd skived a ride off her and was putting her life in danger. But he'd never considered her as more.

She was so…Goth Always in black. She dyed her hair. She wore heavy eye makeup. And she drove a hearse!

But now, here he was in that hearse, and she was helping, while Celia, the perfect pert little girlfriend, was getting a convertible T-bird in return for letting him go and get eaten by a hellhound. Something was very wrong.

"Do you think you can walk now?" Brianna said.

"Yeah. Where are we?" Kelvin realized that they had traveled while he had slept. He didn't know the area.

"Just a place I know." Brianna lowered her window and cocked her head. "It sounds okay. Let's go."

She got out, and he followed. They reached the front door of the seemingly closed shop where Brianna knocked three times, looked around, then knocked three times again. She hummed a few lines of *Knock Three Times* and waited. Kelvin heard a distant howl, setting every hair on his body on edge. It might have only been a dog, but it wasn't. He knew it wasn't. He wanted that door to open, and in a hurry.

The door cracked open, and he brushed past Brianna to get inside.

No one was on the other side waiting for them.

"Um, who opened the—"

Brianna shushed him. "Don't ask questions. Just c'mon in, and let's see what we can find out."

She pushed him in further, then shut the door and threw the deadbolt. She grabbed a saltcellar and sprinkled a line in front of the door. "Better safe than sorry. The books are in the back."

She led him through the dimly lit shop. The walls were lined with…things. Kelvin couldn't identify them, but little tags dangled, their whiteness showing up in the otherwise dark interior. He couldn't read what was written on them, but he was happy about that. If he knew what they said, he might have to leave, and right about now, he didn't want to leave the store. It might be safe. Safer than being outside, anyway.

Brianna pressed a button, and a wall slid aside. "This part isn't open to the general public." They wandered into the room, the light turning on as they walked through the archway.

Kelvin stepped back. "How do these lights keep turning on as we pass them?"

"Motion sensors." She pointed to the light switch, which had a glowing light in it. Brianna laughed. "Did you think it was magic?"

"No, not at all. Okay, sorta."

Brianna kept laughing. "Seriously, magic? To turn on lights?" She shook her head. "Why would we waste it on that?"

The door slid back into place, and again she was quick with the salt, laying a line down where the door would open. She grabbed a few books off the shelf directly in front of her, tossing the top two to Kelvin.

She settled down at the desk and gestured to a recliner in the corner. "Read."

She began flipping through a few pages. Kelvin opened the first book and blanched. The images were hand drawn, and they were of demons, witches, and beheadings. He could swear the woman on the first page looked like Celia.

He kept going. The book dealt with demons and their spawn. Nothing about hellhounds at all. He kept going through the next one. More about demons. The drawings in the second volume were slightly more disturbing. And there was a chapter about hellhounds. He sucked in his breath as he read it. It wasn't good. Only one thing could lure a hellhound away from its purpose—love. And only one thing could bind it—iron.

"We need to get down to the subway. Iron can trap a hellhound."

Brianna looked up at him. "You found something already?"

"Yeah, we gotta get over there. It will follow me, and then it will get bound to the tracks. We can leave it there to get killed by the train."

"Score." Brianna smiled and left her books on the table. She grabbed a thin knife, it looked like a letter opener, and hit another spot in the wall, making the door slide open again. "Let's do it."

They headed to the station, Kelvin studiously ignoring any noises that sounded like dogs or wolves or coyotes. If this worked… if Brianna's book was right…if he made it happen…lots of *ifs*. He didn't like that. But he was willing to try anything to save himself. A snowball's chance in hell was still a chance. Everyone said that one day hell would freeze over, and if it so happened that he brought the snowball down on that day, well, he kept telling himself that it could happen.

***

Brianna parked the hearse, and they walked to the station. Kelvin could see how she gripped the knife, holding it up her sleeve, hidden from anyone who didn't know it was there. He wondered if she was holding it for him, trying to keep him safe.

A man stood in the doorway of the station, open guitar case at his feet, strumming a tune that Kelvin had never heard, singing lyrics that made no sense. The case had a few dollars in it, a bunch of quarters and small change, and roses.

"Dude, those roses for sale?" Kelvin asked.

The guy stopped long enough to nod. "Five bucks, man."

A howl in the distance. It was almost over now, for better or for worse. Kelvin fumbled through his wallet, ignoring Brianna's gestures meant to make him hurry up. He tossed ten dollars in the case and grabbed two roses. The guy singing nodded again. "Thanks, man. Thanks." And he went right back into the nonsensical lyrics and strumming.

Kelvin and Brianna went down the stairs, into the tunnel. Puddles of urine and the stench of unwashed masses came up at them. The subway. Not a place that Kelvin normally went willingly, but this was his only way out, his only chance, the only way he could make it through the night alive.

They got to the tracks. No one else was waiting that night. The last train was due at two, and it was already after 1:30.

Kelvin took Brianna's hand, the one holding the letter opener. He gently removed it from her hand with one hand and handed her a rose with the other.

"You love me, don't you? You always have?"

Brianna took the rose, grasped it in both hands, sniffed it. "Yes. Yes, I always did. I do."

"That's all I needed to know." Kelvin reached toward her, a slow-motion hug, but shifted at the last minute, going from embracing her to shoving her. Hard. Off balance, she stumbled, tripping over the do not cross line and the lip of cement meant to keep anyone from accidentally crossing the line. She went down, her head cracking on the iron rail. She didn't try to stand up…she didn't even move.

Behind him, he could hear the hellhound. It wasn't baying or howling anymore. Now it snuffled along, scenting what he had left for it.

Love.

Love laid on the tracks below him.

The book had been clear; he needed to offer love to the hellhound. The hellhound would scent it, find it, try to take it from him. And then the beast would be trapped on the iron rail, the train would hit it, and Kelvin would be free.

He almost felt guilty. Brianna had only been helping him. But it was her or him. He knew he had the brighter future, had more to offer the world. She was just a Goth.

He stepped to the side, not looking directly at it, but still feeling the heat sloughing off the animal as it shuffled past him. Would it turn to him? Or would it keep going? Had he done everything the right way? It was literally do or die. And he really, really didn't want to die.

The edge of his jeans singed, but didn't catch on fire, and then the hound was down on the track. Kelvin stared straight ahead, ignoring the chewing noises, the groans, the slurping.

The train was coming early. The tracks had begun to vibrate and hum. He heard them singing, and he stared at the lights, at the window in the front car, at the tiled walls around him. Anywhere but down.

The train rumbled in, there were noises he pretended not to hear, noises like when he was a kid and his dog had escaped and gotten onto the highway. Like when the semi had come barreling down the road. Like when his dog flew through the air right in front of him. He didn't notice any of it. Then the train was gone. He stood there, Brianna's knife in one hand, the rose in the other.

Watching the train disappear into the night, he brought the flower to his nose before tossing it to the tracks.

About the author: Katherine Sanger was a Jersey Girl before getting smart and moving to Texas. She's been published in various e-zines and print, including *Baen's Universe, Black Chaos, Wandering Weeds, Spacesports & Spidersilk, Black Petals, Star*Line, Anotherealm,* and *RevolutionSF,* and edited *From the Asylum,* an e-zine of fiction and poetry, and *Serial Flasher,* a flash fiction e-zine. She's a member of HWA and SFWA. She taught English for over 10 years at various online and local community and technical colleges. You can check out links to her many, many blogs at http://www.fromtheasylum.com or find her at Facebook https://www.facebook.com/katherine.sanger.5 or twitter @KatherineSanger.

Jumping In

by C. J. Brooks

Kelvin pressed against the wound as blood seeped around his hands. He felt helpless watching the blood form narrow rivers of continuous red rivulets before dripping onto the floor. Upon entering the train station, he ducked into the men's room, thankful he was alone for the moment. He made an attempt to clean himself up and slow down the blood loss with paper towels. He should have been more careful about choosing someone but there was nothing he could do about that now. Evidently, he had not picked the right one last time anyway.

He had to make an emergency jump, something his father would not have approved of. While gazing into the mirror, he saw the sparkle of bright blue flecks in his eyes and immediately knew it was because the lights in the bathroom had begun to flicker and dim. His eyes were the only thing that could possibly give him away.

He wondered how the man he had been with had gotten into so much trouble so quickly. Nothing during the week he'd been with him had even remotely suggested he was part of a drug cartel or that he was stealing from them. Kelvin had never seen any drugs stashed in his home. He was even more surprised when they attacked him, which forced him into an emergency jump, and well, having this happen.

He lost himself in the moment, staring blankly at nothing until the wincing of pain reminded him of the urgency of his current dilemma. This body would definitely not last long. Glancing into the mirror one last time, and finally satisfied with his appearance, he turned to leave just as an older man came in the door.

"Young man, I think you'd better hurry along."

"What are you talking about?" asked Kelvin, slightly irritated that someone was bothering him. He quickly averted his eyes from the man.

"They called your train, Sir." said the older man motioning to one of his outside pockets.

Kelvin looked down at his pocket, seeing the train ticket he now possessed.

"Oh, right, thank you." He nodded at the man as he hurried out the door.

Kelvin searched for the train he was to board but since there were two and he didn't know which was his, he stopped at the first one, holding out his ticket to one of the men in line. It had become difficult to hear above the noise of the trains but the man shook his head, and then pointed to the second one.

As Kelvin walked toward the other one, he wondered if getting on a train was a good idea, but after seeing the boarding line, he thought it might be his best option since he was in a hurry. After all, he knew nothing about this man, and the ride would give him some time to get his bearings. Maybe he could find someone to choose as a better host without having to make yet another leap of faith. He smiled to himself.

The attendant at the front checked his ticket as he stepped up into the car. He carefully chose one of the seats that would allow him to look at the majority of the other passengers as they boarded and sat down.

Kelvin tried his best to keep to himself as it seemed what

caused the least grief in his life. At 28 years old, he felt life should have gotten easier by now. He loved watching the other passengers. That's why he liked working at the diner on the edge of town. He is interested in all of them, wondering what their lives are like, but he knows by their stares they think he is judging them. He is, but not in the way they think.

Growing up, he never felt as though his life had been his own. Always being told what to wear, what to say, where and when to jump, he had a terrifying time being alone. Now he had no one around to tell him anything. After getting used to it, he had come to like it this way. He knew he couldn't stay long in this body anyway. Even now he could feel it dying. He had to find another one quicker than he had anticipated.

The train began to move, and as Kelvin gazed out the window, he noticed a small grouping of evening primrose growing along the side of the track just as the sun was beginning to set. He could only imagine how beautiful they would be blooming in the moonlight.

He overheard a woman telling her little boy that they would be going into a tunnel in a few minutes and he needed to sit still when the lights dimmed. Kelvin glanced at them briefly, shaking his head. The boy could not have been more than nine or ten years old, jumping in and out of his seat with vibrant energy. While he was considering him, the boy caught him staring.

"What you starin' at, mister? Ain't you ever seen red hair before?"

The boy's mother shushed him, without even glancing Kelvin's way.

Feisty too, Kelvin thought. He liked that. It's too bad using children was frowned upon by his kind. Feeling his body weakening even more he thought about it for another moment then shook it off. To him, it would be absolutely unforgiveable.

Then he noticed him. He was a friendly, athletic looking man, probably around thirty years old, with a bouquet of flowers in his hand. Somehow he had gotten past him without him noticing. Yes, the train was crowded but the man had flowers in his hand and he always noticed flowers. He also noticed the empty seat next to him.

As he walked over to sit beside him, he heard the young mother say "This is it!" He was totally unprepared for the tunnel and dimming lights as it went completely dark for an instant and the emergency lights kicked in.

In that instance, he heard the boy yelling, "What's wrong with his eyes?" While his mother gasped, holding the boy tightly to her.

"Stay away from my child, you freak!"

Even with the commotion, either no one else had seen his eyes or they just didn't care. They may have thought the mother and son were just crazy. Thankfully, the lights came back up just as Kelvin reached the man with the flowers.

"Pardon me, sir." Kelvin said, casually sitting down beside him, smiling and nodding. He had never been a part of someone who loved flowers as much as he did. This could prove to be life altering.

Pressing closer to the man, he said, "I absolutely adore flowers! Who are they for?"

The man pulled the flowers closer to him then smiled apologetically. "They are for me. They will look great on the table in my entryway."

Kelvin thought for a minute. Pressing even closer to the man, he did not hesitate and pierced him with his needle sharp augmented appendage, pumping the poison into him that would allow him to merge with this human. Once he saw the man's eyes glaze over with a fixed stare, he felt his body relax. Kelvin leaned over and whispered, "The flowers will look great on the table in *our* entryway."

Kelvin got off the train at its next stop, completely refreshed. He faintly heard someone scream from inside the train as they found what was left of his last host. He would need to remember this for another time.

Pleased with himself, he admired the fresh flowers he held in his hand and took out the one that looked the strongest. While putting it into his lapel, he thought it was a pity something so beautiful would not last. He held the withered and dying flower for a moment as if reflecting on the evening's events. Watching the train disappear into the night, he brought the flower to his nose before tossing it to the tracks.

About the author: C.J. Brooks is a writer of short horror stories. She currently lives in Georgia with her three dogs, Spike, Xander, and Nikki. This is her first published work.

Stardust

by Ben Eads

Kelvin pressed against the wound as blood seeped around his hands. Switching the drill to reverse and squeezing the trigger, he pulled the rusted bit out of her leg. Her screams pierced his ears. He grinned and stuffed a rag inside the jagged hole.

"My family...they will pay you anything you want!" she said, sobbing. "Let me go. Please, I won't tell anyone. I won't say a thing." Her thin, elegant body struggled against the ropes binding her to the chair, little red rivers dribbling from her wrists, ankles, and neck. "Stop! Please...just, let me go."

"Shhh," Kelvin said, placing a finger on his charred lips. "It will only hurt until I drill *through* the nerve."

Placing his enormous hand on her forehead, he brought the drill-bit close to her eye, settling the tip just below her wet eyelid, and pulled the trigger. Air escaped his lungs, his breath becoming a rattle. Spots danced in front of his eyes.

I'm drowning.

He dropped the drill on the floor.

"Cut! Goddammit, Kelvin," Steve shouted, rising from his director's chair. He marched toward him, balling his hands into pudgy little fists. "What is it now?"

Where's my inhaler?

Kelvin could see the blue pathways of veins on his forehead swell and shrink with every breath Steve took.

"Okay. Here's what's going to happen, you freak. I'm gonna go over there, sit my happy ass in the director's chair, and yell action! And when you hear that, you say the line. Then, we'll get the shot and wrap this piece of shit."

"I…can't…breathe…" Kelvin managed.

Cocking his head, Steve cupped his ear. "Do you hear that, Kelvin? That's the sound of no one giving a flying fuck! I've got a fucking Oscar waiting for me a studio away and couldn't give a flying shit about Splatter Bath 3…but I have to do it for the studio. And you're not helping me here."

"Steve, something's really wrong with him," the special effects guru said, a comforting blur in his peripheral vision that hit Kelvin so hard with a wall of cheap cologne he could taste it.

Squatting next to Kelvin, Dave began pulling the leather suit apart in search of Kelvin's inhaler.

"Where'd you put it, Kelv, huh? Help me out here, buddy."

Kelvin's stilt-like legs gave out. With a smack, his ass hit the fake blood-soaked floor.

"Someone's gotta call 911," Dave said.

Kelvin pulled the inhaler free from a pocket on his hip. He shoved it into his mouth and pressed the button that delivered life.

Thank you, Lord.

"Thank you, Dave. You're a life-saver. I need a minute, okay?"

"Anything—hey, I could go get your oxygen for you. I'll be right back."

"Let me know when your little circle jerk is done, okay?"

"Steve, calm—"

"Answer me one single question, Kelvin," Steve said, waving away Dave's protests. "Who smoked three packs a day? Not me!" Steve pointed at him. "You gave yourself emphysema! And when I found you at that gas station in the middle of piss-poor Nowhere, pushing a mop around, what did I do? I *saved* your ass. And this is how you repay me?" He turned to walk away. "Take thirty!"

Dave glared at the back of Steve's head and ran his hands through his hair. "Are you sure you don't want me to get your oxygen?"

"No, no. Sit for a while with me, okay?"

Dave nodded, wiping sweat from his brow.

"I've killed more people on screen than the common cold." Kelvin held up the inhaler. "But without this, forget it. I'm toast." He managed a short laugh that led to another coughing fit.

"I think it's best I hold it for you. So next time this doesn't happen."

"Thanks," he said, handing the inhaler to him. "I may need you to mail a FedEx envelope to my mama later. Can you do that?"

"Sure, man. Anything."

Kelvin found the folded Polaroid of his mom and caressed it. A tear meandered down the cheek only the woman in the faded picture could understand. He stared at that sweet, supple face that made his childhood bearable, and the lines that endured it.

"This…this is the last picture I took of her. Before…before I got the job here. Without me she'll—"

"Calm down, Kelv," Dave said, placing a hand on his shoulder.

"I've spent the last three years working with him. And when I get her letters—you know what she says? That she's proud. Just once, I'd like to make one movie she could see me in. But my face…"

The spots returned when Kelvin tried to get up. He slumped back down, exhaling.

"Kelvin, you know the film Steve's working on next door?"

Kelvin shook his head.

"Shit…doesn't surprise me. He's kept that thing as tight as his ass. No one knows much. But I do. I think I can make that dream come true for you, buddy. I'll talk to Steve—"

"It's the money I'm worried about, honestly. Mamma hasn't received one check from the studio. And this is the third film. Every day, when everyone else is eating their lunch, I can't help but think of her. It kills me to think of her walking to the mailbox and finding nothing but bills. She's not well, ya' know?"

"Look, I've got to talk to Steve anyway. You just stay here, relax, and I'll go to bat for you, brother. Okay?"

"Okay."

"Don't worry about these assholes, yeah? I've got your back." Dave rose to his feet.

"Dave."

"Yeah?"

"Thanks."

"For what?"

"For being my friend," Kelvin said. "I've never had one before."

Dave's face contorted. "What are friends for?" he said, and did his best to smile as he wiped the tears away before heading off to search for Steve.

Kelvin traced a gnarled fingertip around his mother's face before pocketing the picture. He grabbed hold of the corner of the wall and hoisted himself up.

I need some fresh air.

"One step at a time. One step at a time."

He took deep breaths until his vision cleared. He walked carefully to the exit and out into the crisp night air.

Jasmine and orange blossoms flooded his senses. It reminded him of the pies his mom used to make and bring to church with them every Sunday.

Light from the open window in Steve's trailer outlined a cross on the ground. The breeze left and he could hear Dave's voice.

Curiosity grabbed Kelvin and pulled him closer to the trailer.

"Listen, Steve, I found the right guy for the role."

"Who?"

Kelvin's heart lodged in his throat. He crept towards the window and cocked his ear.

"Me, that's who. Don't worry about any CGI. My team can come up with a suit—and with the right camera angles, we can make it work. But when the mask comes off, you need a face like this. Not like—"

"Kelvin's?" Steve said, and the laughter tore the thin fabric of Kelvin's heart. Fingernails pressed red, crescent moons into his palms.

What are friends for?

Kelvin almost retired to his own trailer then remembered the money. His mother's money. He began to cough again. The taste of copper made his stomach churn.

What did the doctor say? Emo...imb...embolism?

He placed a hand on Steve's trailer to steady himself as the fit took its course. He spat what came up on the ground.

"Is that him?" Steve said.

"Shhh…"

Kelvin took a deep breath and opened the door to Steve's trailer. He noticed Dave sitting at a table, white lines of powder carved out atop a silver platter.

"So, you think you can just waltz in here after that stunt you pulled?"

"I don't mean to cause any trouble, no sir. I just need to talk to you about my payments. You see, my mama hasn't received one since we started. I'm very concerned for her health, sir. Can you help me out?"

Steve chuckled. "Listen, dickhead, that's the studio's problem. Not mine. How many times do I have to repeat myself, huh?"

"Yes, sir, I'm sorry but, I called them and they said I had to talk to you."

"Are you calling me a liar, Kelvin? Is that what you heard,

Dave?"

"I think so."

"Well now, it's unanimous!" Steve said. He cut another line and snorted it.

"Go! And be ready in ten minutes to shoot your final scene. We're done here."

"No disrespect, sir, but I won't do anything until you make that phone call. I'm not a smart one, no sir, but I'm sure if I call the lawyer, the one with the Union, he'd want to have a say in this. You know—the one I called about the merchandising."

The color drained from Steve's face.

"My, oh, my. The boy finally grew a pair of balls. So what are you saying?"

"What's fair is fair," Kelvin said. "My mama needs—"

"How much?"

"Wait." Dave turned to Steve. "You're not going to give this… freak an advance, are you?"

"What? Are you going to call the Union, too?"

Dave bolted from his chair and reached across the table at Steve. His fingertips caught between the buttons of his shirt. They made a popping sound as Dave pulled.

"Let go!" Steve yelled as he grabbed for the phone. "Security—"

Kelvin halved the distance between them and grabbed Dave's wrist, squeezing until he screamed.

Taking the inhaler from him and placing it in his pocket, Kelvin let him go. Dave swung wild, but Kelvin placed his large palm on Dave's forehead, bringing him to a dead stop.

"Wait! Wait right there," Steve said, framing them up for a shot with his hands. "That's perfect. Dave, you're done. Let's see daddy get you outta this one."

"Oh, come on! You're not serious about this. Who's going to play the lead then?"

"Kelvin, how would you like to be in a real movie for once?"

"You give my mama what she deserves and we'll talk."

I may not be smart, but mama didn't raise no fool.

"Of course, Kelvin. Just escort Dave out of my trailer, will ya?"

"Yes, sir," Kelvin said as he maneuvered Dave through the door and outside.

"Let me go!"

"Dave, I'm sorry. In the good book it says not to hurt another—"

"If you think for a moment you're getting away with this... you're just as dumb as you look."

Kelvin watched two shadows move from the side of the trailer and grab a hold of Dave.

Steve opened the door to his trailer and stepped outside. "That's him, boys, and I want him off the premises!" He turned to Kelvin. "I'm sorry about that, Kelvin. Here's your check. We'll get you in costume next door. It's the last shot where Mary-Bell unmasks her secret admirer before she leaves the train station for the Red Cross. You're wrapped for tonight and we'll just go ahead and get a new call-time for your shots tomorrow, okay?"

"Yes, sir."

"Dave was right, Kelvin. You're not very smart but you've got balls. Dave had been up my ass for weeks over this part—the unmasked lead. I thought about *you*...but it wasn't until tonight. And for once, you've made me happy. Look, I'll walk you over to the set, okay?"

"Yes, sir."

"Cut the sir shit, okay?"

"Okay."

"Now, this is where real movies are made," Steve said, opening the door. "We've got to get you in wardrobe."

Kelvin felt his jaw go slack, taking in the sheer audacity. The sets, the lights, and the superstars below them. For a moment, the magic was real. Kelvin shook his head just to make sure it wasn't the emphysema stealing his breath.

"Kelvin, I'd like you to meet, Stacey. She's head of wardrobe."

"Ma'am."

"Steve, what's going on?"

"I found *him*, Stacey. This is our new man. Well, our un-masked man."

Kelvin's neck and cheeks became warm from her stare.

"Stacey, we don't have to do much, do we? I mean with the coat, we just have to—"

"Not much at all. The coat will hide everything. Here, try this on for size."

"Yes, ma'am."

Kelvin slid into a dark, suede coat. He traced the supple leather with his gnarled hands.

So this is what a real coat feels like.

"How does it fit, Stacey?"

"Like a glove," she said and had Kelvin do a turn-around in front of Steve.

"Is Kelvin ready?"

"You tell me, boss."

"Perfect! Okay, let's wrap this, shall we?"

"Here," Stacey said. She held out a mask that another, more handsome actor wore only weeks before. An actor he watched steal the hearts of countless women in movies. Real movies, like the kind his mama watched, with him sitting next to her on the floor of their little trailer. Kelvin took the mask and slid it on.

Oh, no...another mask. Mama won't see me if...

Kelvin pulled out the FedEx envelope from inside his Splatter Bath suit, slipped the check inside and sealed it. He walked past the mirrors and the myriad of faces that filled them, toward the FedEx Pickup sign and placed it atop the other packages.

Well, mask or no mask, Mama, you'll see me.

"Consider yourself lucky," Stacey said.

"Ma'am?"

"Not many men have kissed Holly Becker."

"Holl…Holly Becker?" Kelvin shivered—the cold seemed to reach all the way through his skin and into his heart. He began wringing his hands. "I…I get to kiss her?"

"Kelvin!" Steve said.

"Here," Stacey said. "This way."

She led him onto a set populated with people dressed just like everyone in the pictures his mama would show him from the old books she kept in her closet. The back of what looked like an actual boxcar was flanked by a dirt road and multitudes of people hustling and bustling by.

"Kelvin!"

"Yes, sir," Kelvin said, walking onto the set. The whole place began to swim in front of him as a coughing fit rose in the back of his throat. Spots danced in his vision again, the familiar tang of pennies flushing across his tongue. People steadied him, one slapping him on the back.

"Kelvin, are you okay?" Steve said.

Where's my inhaler?

Kelvin coughed again and when his eyes adjusted he saw Stacey's pretty face below his with little crimson dots.

I'm drowning!

"Kelvin? Oh, no," Steve said as he rushed toward him. "Where did you put it?"

Kelvin reached underneath the coat and padded the leather, searching. Shaking fingers found it in one of his pockets. He pulled it out and brought it to his lips and pushed the trigger. Nothing.

What are friends for?

"Kelvin, I pulled a lot of strings tonight."

"I'm…I'm fine."

No you're not.

"Do you need some time?"

Kelvin felt the spongy tissue make its way up his bronchial tubes and stick. Some made it into his mouth. He spat the pieces on the ground.

"Nope. I'm good. What's my line?"

Steve explained the scene and lines as Kelvin held back another cough.

"Quiet on set!" Steve said, and the studio became silent. "First positions!"

"Kelvin," Stacey whispered. "After Steve says action, walk up to the end of the boxcar and wait for Holly to come out."

Kelvin made an okay sign with his hand.

Gonna make you proud, Mamma.

"Rolling," Steve said. "Slate in. Action."

Kelvin took his place on the train track beneath Holly, a woman he had only seen on the covers of newspapers and magazines. Despite Holly being dressed like a man and wearing a fake mustache to hide from whoever the bad guys were, he could still make out her form: her elegance, her sincerity.

"I can't hide with you like this...I can't keep it up," she said. "They almost killed you, Max. For something I haven't even seen. You never showed me—"

"Can I have one last kiss?" Kelvin said, hoping the sweat wasn't that noticeable on his forehead.

"Only if I can see your face. The face that..."

Kelvin removed his mask. Holly brought her hand to her mouth and gasped. "Who did this to you?"

Kelvin reached up, placed his hand on the back of her head and threaded his fingers through her golden locks. He took one last deep breath and tasted a mouth he only knew in dreams. Electricity surged up his spine.

"My father...he tried to burn the house down when mama was away." Kelvin said, feeling the phantom flames engulfing his body all over again. "I'm sorry."

"That's not his line," Steve whispered. "Just…go with it."

The color drained from Holly's face. She paused, jaw agape. "Come for me," she said as the tears spilled down her face.

The boxcar came to life and began to move down the tracks.

Kelvin let out his breath, holding onto the aftertaste. He tried pulling another but his system began to fail.

"I love you, Mama," he said.

A protruding tulip on the ground reminded him of his mama's garden. He plucked it. The spots returned and he floated inside, like the time he broke a tooth and had to see Doctor Winn, who gave him the gas that made him feel woozy, and then made his tummy sick. But only this time he stayed woozy and his tummy wasn't sick. It was fine. He felt nothing. Nothing but Holly's kiss on his lips and the emptiness of breath.

Finally, you'll have some money, Mama. And don't worry, you'll see me again, as many times as you like on TV…

Watching the train disappear into the night, he brought the flower to his nose before tossing it to the tracks.

About the author: Ben Eads lives within the semi-tropical suburbs of Central Florida. A true horror writer by heart, he wrote his first story at the tender age of ten. Ben has had short stories published in various magazines and anthologies. When he isn't writing, he dabbles in martial arts, philosophy, and specializes in I.T. security. He's always looking to find new ways to infect a reader's imagination. Ben blames Arthur Machen, H.P. Lovecraft, Jorge Luis Borges, J.G. Ballard, Philip K. Dick, and Stephen King for his addiction, and his need to push the envelope of fiction. His critically acclaimed horror novella, *Cracked Sky* is available on Amazon.com

Purple Eclipse

by Cynthia Dawn Griffin

Kelvin pressed against the wound as blood seeped around his hands. "Damn Old-Timer! You shot me, ya fu—"

"Kelvin, let's get outta here!" Kayla screamed.

Her heart pounded like the booming base of Kelvin's car woofers. She hadn't seen the gun until it was too late. One second the old man behind the counter held his hands up, and the next a revolver came to aim on her twin. The shot sent a rainstorm of Momma's Best potato chips showering down on them, but the bullet must have grazed Kelvin, too. A dark, wet spot stained his black hooded jacket. He kept one hand on his side as he jerked his own gun from his coat pocket, aiming it at the old man.

Kayla backed toward the door with a crumpled plastic shopping bag clutched in her hand. The money should have gone in it, but that was before the crazy clerk surprised them. Kayla only wanted out. She pulled at her brother's arm, but he shoved her off, causing Kayla to stumble to the floor.

A stabbing pain raced up her knee from where it impacted the concrete. She struggled to get up, fighting the tears that stung her eyes. She stopped mid squat as she came face to face with a little girl who clung to a tiny purple flower, matching her lacy lilac dress.

"Lena!" A woman shrieked as she attempted to grab the dazed

girl.

Another boom echoed in the small store. Something stung Kayla's cheek, and then the little girl crumbled to the floor. Kayla watched too shocked to move or breath as a red stain spread across the girl's purple lacy chest. The tiny flower fell from the girl's fist and tumbled to the grimy floor.

"No!" Kayla reached to help the girl.

But Kayla was jerked away and out the store's front door. Sirens splintered the rainy night. Kayla struggled to go back. A sharp sting hit her already throbbing cheek. She looked up into the blazing eyes of her brother.

"Stop messin' around. The 5-0 are coming. We need to jet." Kelvin's voice drowned out the wailing sirens, but only for a moment.

"The girl—"

"Fuck the girl. We have to go. Now!"

Kayla glared after her brother through the drizzle of rain as she watched him race to their getaway car in a handicap spot. He slid in the driver's seat, gunning the engine. "Let's go!"

His voice was like a fist to her gut, and it spurred her into action. Jumping in, she reached for the door as the old Buick lurched backward. The stench of burning rubber wafted in through her open window. Red and blue lights cut through the thick night and her stomach clinched. Maybe they would be in time to save that poor girl.

"Shit!" Kelvin said.

They barreled out of the Twin Tires Stop N' Go parking lot. Kayla gripped the sides of her seat and said a prayer. She had confidence in her brother. He could out-pace anything with wheels, but noticed the sweat beading on his forehead as the streetlights threw eerie patterns across his face.

"You're hurt," Kayla said.

"No shit!"

"Why do you have to be so mean?"

Kelvin gave her a surprised look. "You want to talk 'bout this now! I can't be jawing at you while I'm making our getaway, littl' sis. Sew it up so I can get us outta here!"

Kayla sat back, noticing the hard line of his jaw and knew from experience that he'd take his anger out on her later. Kayla had enough bruises to testify to that. But that had been her fault for being stupid enough to make him mad. Kelvin was a nice guy. He just had a temper. She knew better than to provoke him.

The town whizzed past her window at a frightening speed, the dark buildings nothing more than a blur. The blaring horns of other cars they passed a chilling music to their escape. Kayla felt like she might be sick. She brought her hand to her mouth in hopes of stopping the nastiness she felt building in her belly. Something rough brushed her lips. Kayla looked down to see she held the little girl's flower.

She remembered the face of the girl, the fear those innocent eyes held as she lay trembling and gushing blood. Kayla brought the flower to her nose to smell it, only to find the flower odorless except for a slight metallic scent. Blood. It stained one of the delicate paper petals. She grasped the flower as if holding it tighter might somehow fix the terrible thing that had happened.

"You think she'll be okay don't you, Kelvin?"

"Who?"

"That little girl."

"How the fuck should I know?" Kelvin turned the steering wheel sharply to the left, sending them careening around a corner.

The sirens seemed closer now. Kayla closed her eyes. How many more times would she have to do this? How many robberies? How many more beatings from her brother? She had been happy in the foster home where she'd been placed after Momma died. The only sad thing was they'd separated her and Kelvin. When he showed up begging her to come with him, she never looked back.

What had Momma always said? *Family is all ya got.*

Kayla owed her brother. He kept her safe and made sure they had food in their bellies. He was the one with the brains who thought of the idea to rob small stores in the first place, but this had been the first time anyone had died.

She shivered. Before Momma died and Pappa had gone away upstate, things had been simpler. Momma always said family was important no matter what happened. A person had to stand by their family, because no one else would. However, when Kayla looked at her family now—Kelvin—she couldn't feel the warm closeness that used to be there. All she saw was a killer just like Pappa.

Kayla flew into the dashboard, slamming her head on the hard surface as the car screeched to a halt. Bright lights flickered in her vision, her head exploding in pain. She couldn't stop the tears from escaping or the sob from passing her lips. Kelvin hated when she cried. But it hurt so much. Kelvin opened the door and yanked her from the car.

The bridge was up. Must have been why they'd stopped in the middle of the road. The cops would be there long before they could cross it, so the two of them abandoned their rusted out Buick with both doors ajar and the lights shining onto the dark Somansh River.

"Why you do have to be such a damn baby?" Kelvin said.

"I'm sorry." Kayla made an effort to stop crying, but her sniffles sounded loud in the stillness of the dark.

They started down the river's bank, leaving the sirens at their backs. A steady shower of rain poured down now. Kayla slipped and landed hard on her side. Hot pain exploded through her body. She stumbled to her feet with difficulty to find Kelvin had disappeared in the moonless night. She held her aching ribs as anxiousness ate at her belly. Where had he gone?

"Kelvin!"

A dark shadow jogged back to her. Relief flooded Kayla at seeing her brother. He hadn't left her. But her joy turned to terror as she saw the fire in his eyes. Kayla knew what happened when he got *that* look. It was the same look Pappa would get before hitting Momma. The smack of Kelvin's open palm upon her flesh sounded almost as bad as the crack of the gun back at that shop. The searing pain mingled with her already throbbing head. A sick dizziness swept through her.

"What the hell you doin'!" Don't you get the trouble we're in?"

"The trouble *you're* in," Kayla whispered. She trembled in shock that she'd been so bold.

Kelvin's eyes were like round fiery double moons. "What the hell is that supposed to mean?"

Kayla didn't want to respond. She didn't want to say the words, but could feel them stuck like peanut butter on the roof of her mouth. A weight as if she'd been carrying that little girl on her back since the moment she'd seen the red spot on the lilac dress, crushed the breath from Kayla's lungs. She knew even though she hadn't been the one to pull the trigger, that girl would follow Kayla for the rest of her life.

"You killed her, Kelvin. No one was ever supposed to get hurt. That's what you told me when we started this. You promised!" The last sentence came out as a wail.

Kelvin ran a hand through his hair. His eyes scanned the night as if some demon might jump out and maul him right then and there. Kayla felt it, too, the hot breath of the demon ready to devour her soul.

"No, I didn't! That old man at the store did. His revolver killed her. It's his fault, not mine."

"But she'd be fine if we'd never gone into that store."

He shook his head. "We have to get moving. The pigs are coming."

Tears were at the corners of Kayla's eyes. She was determined not to cry again. "I can't. I hurt too much." Her sides throbbed and she felt the burn of her cheek as the rain slapped her skin, but it was the torment inside that ached the most.

"Dammit. I'm the one bleeding here. Come on!"

He grabbed her hand and pulled, but Kayla refused to move. "I said, no."

That familiar dark look crossed his face. Kayla braced herself, but Kelvin seemed to be in thought.

"Fine," he said. "It might be better if we split up." He licked his lips and nodded. "Yeah, that's a good idea. We split up and make them chase us both. It will give us a better chance of gettin' away." He looked back into the night where the sirens howled like angry beasts. "We need somewhere to meet. How about the train station? There's a midnight train going to Atlanta. We could catch it and leave this place behind. We could start new, and I promise no more killing, and…" He caressed the side of her cheek that still burned from his slap. "And I promise I won't hit ya no more."

A ghost of regret crossed his features. A trickle of hope burst through her heart as Kayla dared to think he might be able to change, but the regret disappeared and Kelvin's jawline hardened once again. Her hope shriveled and died. And a terrible realization came to Kayla as she stood there in the gushing rain with her heart soaking wet with the truth. Kelvin was just like Pappa and she was just like Momma. A circle of hopelessness that could never be broken.

Kayla let herself smile, even though she didn't feel it. "That sounds good, Kelvin. A new start."

He smiled back. "Yes, a new start for you and me." He wrapped her into a quick embrace and then stepped back. "We have to move, littl' sis. You go that way." He pointed away from the river to a cluster of darkened storefronts, stuffing a few dollars into her hand. "I'll follow the river down more. Once you get to the street, find a cab or a bus to take you to the station. I don't know if they've identified us yet, but put this hat on so they can't see your face." He pulled out his faded Carhartt hat from his back pocket and slapped it on her head.

Kayla felt something catch in her throat. "Kelvin, I love you."

"Hush, littl' sis. Now go." Kelvin said with a softness Kayla had rarely ever seen her brother show.

The look made Kayla's insides twist up in a jumbo sized pretzel. Kelvin gave something to her he loved. That silly old hat had gone through a lot—almost as much as they had. It had been a gift from Pappa a few months before he'd accidentally killed Momma after getting drunk one night. It had been the one thing Kelvin kept, while leaving everything else behind. He loved that hat and it made her think maybe he might truly love her, too. And here she had nothing to give him in return. She looked down in shame and glimpsed the purple flower still held tightly in her fist.

"Wait." Kayla stuffed the purple flower in his hand. The paper was mostly crushed now, but there was the faintest evidence it once might have been a flower. The spot of blood seemed to be the only thing that stood untouched, a perfect circle of red on the crumbled purple paper. "Here. You can give it back when you see me next."

He gave her a strange look. "What's this?"

"You gave me something of yours. Now you have something of mine."

Kelvin carelessly shoved the flower in his pocket and turned to round the bend of the riverbank. Kayla watched his receding form underneath the half-moon now peeking its pale face from the dark clouds. The rain had stopped, but she could feel a dankness surround her heart.

***

Kayla stood under the cover of trees as she watched the train from her hidden spot. She made it to the station without much trouble. She caught a cab and arrived half an hour ago. She had gone up to the ticket office and even purchased her ticket, but hadn't been able to get on the train. She had walked around until she found a small alcove in the shadow of night so she could get away from the prying eyes of the other travelers at the station.

She needed time to think. Should she get on the train and start a new life with her twin, even though in her heart she knew nothing would change? Or should she stay here and take her chances with the cops? Kayla couldn't remember seeing any cameras at the shop, so maybe she could stay here and return to her foster family. She really liked them, and now felt more than a little angry at Kelvin for taking her away from people who seemed to care about her.

Family is all ya got. But couldn't family be something more than blood?

Kayla glimpsed Kelvin on the platform. Afraid he might see her, she fell further back into the shadows. He dashed past people to get to the train, but the doors closed leaving him behind. The train began to move out of the station in slow motion. Her brother stood with a defeated look on his face. Kayla's eyes fell to a splash of purple tightly grasped in his fist. He still had her gift. Her heart warmed and the desire to go to him strummed in her veins. But as Kayla put a step forward the haunting image of the dying little girl made her stop.

Kayla stared at the tiny flower as if it might sprout into a demon that would devour her at any moment. Tears flowed down her cheeks freely, washing away the last bit of her doubt. She knew with every part of her she couldn't go to him. As much as it hurt, she was done with her brother. She was ready to break the cycle.

She heard her momma's rebuke chide her. *He's your brother, Kayla.* Kayla shook her head. *Yeah, Momma, but sometimes family hurts are too deep. Look at where it got you.* Momma didn't answer. Her chiding voice and stern face disappeared in the blackness of Kayla's mind.

A group of uniformed cops converged on the train station. Kelvin hadn't seen them yet. Kayla turned to leave, but before she did she gave her twin one last long look.

Watching the train disappear into the night, he brought the flower to his nose before tossing it to the tracks.

About the author: Cynthia "Dawn" Griffin is self-employed, working on all manner of fun stuff from writing, editing, and even likes to design a book cover every now and again. She lives in Maryland with her husband and son. Some of her hobbies include: photography, graphic design, reading, movies, yoga, and spending time lounging on her front porch drinking wine. She also has a weakness for all things chocolate. Dawn loves writing speculative fiction, science fiction, and non-fiction, and is currently working on a science fiction fantasy novel series. You can find out more about her at cynthiagriffin.wordpress.com

Fixing a Broken Shadow

by Marty Young

Kelvin pressed against the wound as blood seeped around his hands.

Another gunshot echoed through the woods. Dirt exploded two feet from him. He ducked back behind the fallen moss-covered tree and, still with one hand pressed to his side, scurried backwards, down the slope, trying not to lose his footing, trying not to scream.

But the dead leaves on the ground were slippery and his feet shot out from under him. He tried to stop his slide, grasping for trees, for branches, for anything. He felt the wound in his side rip wider and now he did cry out. He doubled up and rolled the rest of the way towards the forested floor twenty feet below.

The world went out, but it was back in mere heartbeats, back with jagged edges and blazing heat. Kelvin pushed himself to his feet. His balance was off and he staggered sideways until he found a tree to keep him up. He gritted his teeth, drew a deep raging breath, and tried again.

Somewhere behind him, he heard a scrabbling among the bush as the man followed him down into the ravine.

He could feel blood dribbling down his leg.

"C'mon," he said, shaking his head to clear it. His steps were heavy but he made good progress, twisting and turning and forcing his way through shrubbery and over fallen trees the best he could until the sounds of pursuit behind him grew distant.

Kelvin stopped and removed his shirt to wrap it around his stomach. He pulled it tight and nearly screamed again. The bullet had passed clean through, which had to be some blessing, right?

"Fuck knows," he said, heading off once more.

The woods were thick and getting thicker, the trees towering high above him, their lower limbs broken and jutting. Rich green moss was everywhere—in places it coated whole trees and hung like vines, and brought with it the scent of mowed grass and sweat. It was a heady mix, and getting stronger.

He pushed on but soon slowed when he spotted the clearing. He looked behind him, listening, but heard nothing. He turned to the clearing again, it was twenty feet across, ringed with trees, and there was a wooden stake in the middle of that clearing, poking a couple of inches above the ground.

It took him a moment to realize the pain in his side was lessoning. He looked down. The blood had stopped flowing. The pain continued to weaken, and then it was gone. He touched the wound, prodded it when touching elicited nothing. Still it didn't hurt.

"Okay..." he said. He looked at the stake again, and then stepped towards it.

"It marks the burial spot of a convict," someone said on his left, causing him to yelp and stagger away from the voice.

There was a bald man next to the huge trunk of a Douglas fir. He wore rolled up pants and a shirt rolled up at the sleeves, both of which might have been blue at one time but were now muddied and stained and torn. His feet were bare, his face moon-round, his eyes small, widely-spaced. He was smiling, too.

"Who're you?" Kelvin asked him.

"Oh," the man said, waving away the question. "Just a man with a broken shadow."

Kelvin couldn't help it, he looked. The man laughed.

"Too much shade to see that, I'm afraid."

"The man with the broken shadow," repeated Kelvin. "I know that from somewhere."

"That stake," the man said. "There's a convict buried there. He was staked through the heart a long time ago so his sin-filled body could never rise from the grave."

Kelvin said nothing.

"He was an evil person, killed three young girls after doing horrid things to them. He was sentenced to death. He was beheaded, then staked through his black heart. They made sure to leave part of the stake poking above ground, Kelvin, so everyone would remember what the loss of innocence looked like."

The old man's eyes shone, catching what little light got through the canopies high above them and reflecting it at Kelvin, who raised his hands in submission.

"It's not what you think," he said, wondering, had he told the man his name?

"I'm sure it's not."

It was a spur of the moment decision, made through desperation. Sure, now, after having been shot and chased and confronted by this strange man with the broken shadow, it was clearly the *wrong* decision, but he had seen the ring tumble to the ground, bouncing with a delicate sound and rolling towards him like it wanted him to bend down and scoop it up, and take it away. Only when he had straightened again, his eyes had caught on those of the man being beaten, being so violently attacked, and there had been such pleading in those eyes.

But Kelvin had turned his back on that despair and walked away, back the way he had come. Slowly at first, but he had soon enough been spurred on by the commotion behind him, the footsteps and yelling, the threats and then the gunshots.

"Clifford Owen," said the man before him now. "That was

his name. Once a self-made man but his life was in tatters when you met him. He was coming to return the ring when the attack happened. Coming to seek forgiveness, as if I could give it. Did you see the desperation in his eyes when you took the ring?"

Kelvin looked down at his hand, the ring looked expensive. Gold, with diamonds studded through its wide band in a swirling pattern.

"He died as a result of that attack."

How much was the ring worth? A lot, probably. Could pawn it for enough dough to keep him in feed and drink for some time. He looked up at the man, at his slight smile, his hungry eyes.

"This ain't yours," Kelvin said. "You're just another hobo like me, like that Clifford guy, lookin' for some easy money."

The man's smile went nowhere. "Oh, I don't want the ring. But think about the stake, Kelvin, and what it represents. That man made a decision, too. Is this the path you want to take?"

"Go find your own ring," Kelvin said as he backed from the clearing.

That smile, all snakes and spiders and darkened corners...

There were sounds behind him now, of snapping twigs and swear words. The man with the gun was back again. Oh joy.

So Kelvin turned and ran, slapping away branches that tried to take out his eyes, and jumping over fallen branches that wanted to trip him over. He ran downslope and then up again, and the sounds behind him never grew any louder. He ran, and continued to run until he found the train tracks that had always led through his life.

The ring was warm around his finger but it was a comforting sensation, one that spread up his arm and down through his torso. His wounded side tingled. He looked down, removed his shirt, and saw unblemished skin.

***

The train tracks zippered his life together, and Kelvin followed the tracks that were covered in grass and long since last used down from the foothills of the Coastal Range, and north through Parkton, keeping to the shadows and the alleyways, where he wouldn't be seen. He trod the newer sleepers as he made his way north through the Willamette Valley, deviating only to find food, or employment.

But no one was hiring and food was scarce. Worse than ever, it seemed. Even the trash cans were empty.

Just north of Parkton, he made a decision and found a pawnbroker. The bell above the door of Trogan's had jingled like laughter when he pushed it open, and he couldn't help but think of that man with the broken shadow's unsettling smile.

Kelvin spotted someone behind the counter and headed towards him. The shop was cluttered with TVs and videos, DVD players, radios and stereos, skis and ski boots, sports gear and shoes and clothes.

"Help you?" The man asked, his hands resting on the glass counter. Beneath the glass top were hunting knives. They looked sharp and dangerous, and the man's forefinger on his left hand lightly scratched against the glass as if anxious to get to the knives below.

Kelvin held up his hand and showed off the ring. He didn't want to take it off but now, he wasn't so sure that was the best idea. "How much for this?"

The man squinted at the band around Kelvin's finger. One side of his mouth curled upwards. "Who'd you steal that from, huh?"

Kelvin lowered his hand as an image of Clifford Owen's pleading eyes flashed across his mind.

"No way a bum like you would own somethin' like that."

Before Kelvin could do anything other than stare, the man pulled out an old pistol. "How 'bout you hand it over so I can find its rightful owners, eh?"

"It's not yours."

"Nope, not yours neither. But figurin' I got the gun, I reckon you can give it to me, right?"

Kelvin nodded. He nodded again. But when he tried to remove the ring, it wouldn't come. He looked from the man with the gun to the knives beneath the glass.

"Looks like we're gonna have t' try one of these fellas."

Without thinking, Kelvin turned and ran. He expected the gun to spit at him and send him down but while he heard it go off, he reached the door and jerked it open without feeling any impact. He glanced back once as he left the store, only to see the man pulling the trigger and the gun smoking, but still he felt nothing.

"*What the fuck?*" the man yelled, but Kelvin didn't wait around to find out.

Safe again in the woodlands surrounding town, Kelvin took off his jacket, and stared at the bullet holes in the back of it. He removed his shirt and saw the same there, too. He didn't want to check his back so he dressed again and tried not to think about it, just like he tried not to look down at the old wound in his side.

Sometimes, those train tracks were scars that would never fade, no matter how they were hidden.

***

"Hey pops," a young kid said one night as Kelvin tried to get comfortable amongst soggy cardboard boxes and piles of newspapers deep down the throat of an alleyway in some other town. The fella had an air about him, one that spoke of quiet confidence and strength. "That's a juicy looking ring you've got there. It sure as hell sparkles."

Kelvin swallowed hard.

The kid pulled out a knife, its blade bright in the dim light of the alleyway. The blade sang, too, faint words Kelvin couldn't quite understand but he could hear the rhythm, like a sad melody. A blues from the heart, singing to him.

"C'mon then, Gollum," said the kid. "Hand it over and I won't make it hurt."

"But I can't get it off," Kelvin said, tugging at the ring on his finger. It caught on his knuckle and wouldn't move any higher up his finger.

"Too bad for you, huh?"

It was all a blur after that. The kid came in fast and swinging the handle of the knife, clutched in one fist, against Kelvin's head, and there'd been stars, so many instant stars, and buzzing, too. He was hit in the head again, and then, as he toppled forward and the world flickered, threatening to go out, he saw the kid, who wasn't a kid, really, because there were too many lines on his face, but as the kid moved in with the blade this time, a distant voice called, "Hey! What the hell's going on down there?"

The kid swore. He looked at Kelvin, then back down the alley. "Goddamn lucky day," he said before disappearing down the alley and into its darkness.

At times like that, Kelvin was sure he could hear the man with the broken shadow offering to take the ring from him, promising all his bad luck would end if he did that one thing. And during such times, Kelvin also thought he could feel the man with the broken shadow savoring the agony of his terror, enjoying its succulence.

Another night, after another attempted mugging, Kelvin thought again about Clifford Owen, the man he had let die. He stared at the cuts on his dirty hands and the bruises on his arms, he felt the stab of pain in his ribs, and he made a decision.

"I'm sorry," he whispered to the man haunting him.

***

The trek back to Parkton, and then beyond, back into those hills and tall imposing trees and their tangle of moss, took him two weeks. He kept off the main roads and that made the way longer, but it was safer doing that. The days were a trial and the nights were agony, hunger ate him hollow and it was only dirty rainwater that kept him going.

The stake called to him like birdsong, guiding him through the woods, and he stumbled into the clearing late one afternoon as the sun sank low. He fell to the ground before the stake, remembering what the man with the broken shadow had told him about the loss of innocence.

He had lost the last of his here, had lost his humanity when he had let someone die. He wondered if he could reclaim it, now.

"Hello?" He croaked. There was no answer. He called again, but only the birds sung back.

When he tugged on the ring, it came off easy, slipping off as if it wanted to go. Kelvin held it up before him. He peered through the hole in its middle but saw no magic there, only trees.

He knelt down and placed the ring on the ground, near the stake.

The moment his fingers lost their touch with the ring, pain exploded in his side, in his back, through his ribs and jaw and the back of his head. Kelvin screamed and fell over, but that only caused the agony in his back to increase, and when he writhed about, his broken ribs cut through his skin and his lungs, and the ancient wound in his side pulled open and bled stagnant blood

"Would you like me to heal you?"

The words, when they came, were so soft, so gentle, that Kelvin thought they were inside his head. It was only when a hand pressed against his blazing chest and dulled the pain that he could grasp air and focus on the face above him.

The man with the broken shadow smiled down at him. "I can heal you, you know."

Kelvin tried to speak but couldn't.

"You fronted up to your deed, and for that, I will take it from you."

As soon as the words were spoken, all of his pain and suffering vanished. Kelvin gasped, then let out the air in a gush before dragging in another.

"Innocence can never be reclaimed," said the man with the

broken shadow. He was fatter now, his clothes ill-fitting, and he was holding the ring, but Kelvin noticed he didn't put it on. Instead, he slipped it into a pocket. "But from that loss grows something new."

When the man withdrew his hand, he held in it a rosebud, its closed petals deep purple, almost black. As Kelvin stared at it, the flower began to open and a rich, sweet scent filled the clearing.

"Come," the man said, offering his hand.

Kelvin took it and climbed to his feet. He checked his side but all that remained of the reborn wound was a bloodstain. His back no longer hurt, nor his chest. He stared at the man before him.

"Let's walk," the man said, and they did.

The path they followed was dirt, barely three feet wide, with old growth Douglas firs standing to either side and casting shadows across their way. Soon, they left the woods and came to the train tracks that had been Kelvin's constant. These were unused, the weeds trying to bury them, but they would need longer to achieve that. Wildflowers nestled against the rails, with jasmine and crocus, pink camellias and multi-colored tulips.

The man with the broken shadow offered Kelvin the rose and he took it.

"Innocence can never be reclaimed, as I said, but in its wake grows maturity, and that is a far more beautiful flower."

There was a rumble in the distance.

"I don't understand any of this," said Kelvin.

"You don't need to understand, only how to be. And you're learning, Kelvin."

Now, the unmistakable sound of a train approached on these weed-filled tracks. Kelvin stared along them, and soon the black mutant face of an old locomotive appeared around the bend, a billow of steam announcing its presence as it surged from the darkness. The train was glowing, radiating from within.

"I know who you are," said Kelvin as the train approached them. "I remember the nursery rhyme."

Marty Young

The man's shadow broke
On his long way down
And monsters grew up
From unhallowed ground

The man smiled. "Only I didn't create the monsters."

"We created them ourselves, didn't we?"

"You *are* the monsters. That's what happens when you lose your humanity. Me? I'm just there to savor it when it happens. Beware the world, Kelvin. You mean so very little, but so very much can be accomplished by something so small. Don't become a monster."

The train roared past, and the man with the broken shadow struck out a hand and the train caught him and took him away.

Kelvin stared at the flower in his hand, its petals already curling up. One dropped off and fell silently to the ground, followed by another. Even the stem was beginning to wilt. But that was okay, he'd remember, just like those who saw the stake.

He went to the rails and stood on the sleepers, which continued to vibrate. Watching the train disappear into the night, he brought the flower to his nose before tossing it to the tracks.

About the author: Marty Young (www.martyyoung.com) is an award-winning writer and editor, and sometimes ghost hunter. His debut novel, 809 Jacob Street, won the Australian Shadows Award for best horror novel in 2013. Marty was the founding president of the Australian Horror Writer's Association from 2005-2010, and one of the creative minds behind the internationally acclaimed Midnight Echo magazine, for which he also served as executive editor until mid-2013. His short horror fiction has been nominated for numerous awards, reprinted in a year's best anthology, and repeatedly included in year's best recommended reading lists, while his essays on horror literature have been published in journals and university textbooks in Australia and India.

Playtime's End

by Nicole E. Castle

Kelvin pressed against the wound as blood seeped around his hands. He squirmed on the Speedtrain's cold tracks—wrists and ankles bound. The sky was full of colors as the sun slowly rose.

"Playtime's over, isn't it, Kelvin?" I asked.

***

They named me Allie, Happy Household Model 234901.

Kelvin Smythe purchased me for his 42nd birthday. He re-named me Mariah, after his mother. By the year 2034, Japan had perfected the first synthetic humans who flooded the market becoming new additions in millions of households across the world—maids, nannies, consultants, partners—sexual and otherwise.

Kelvin never had the means but always the want.

After receiving forgiveness from an elderly aunt for accidentally killing her pet mongoose when he was 16, she left him a hefty inheritance. The first thing he bought was me.

On the showroom floor, the salespeople expounded how "extravagant and perfect" we are.

"She can play the hell out of the zither and recite Shakespeare and Dante line-for-line. Beyond that, she does what every other human woman does. She cleans, she sweeps, she cooks, she gardens, she sucks…," he paused, jabbing Kelvin in the ribs, "and she fucks like a pro. This model does it all with a smile and a grace no human woman possesses or ever could." Kelvin was hooked.

He brought me home and treated me very well, at first. He even helped do the dishes some nights. He was a considerate lover, although, I had been prepped for any kink, fetish, or other deviant behavior my owner might desire. Kelvin treated me as an equal.

***

On the night of our sixth month anniversary, Kelvin has an idea. What would a butter knife inside of me feel like? Kelvin was born with strange notions. He confessed one evening that his aunt's mongoose was an unfortunate accident. He had hoped to have much more fun with the beast, but it proved too fragile.

"Come to me, Mariah. Time to play!" As he fucks me repeatedly with the butter knife, I keep the same smile on my face, repeating the 'In the Bedroom' phrases I was programmed with, "Kelvin, you make me feel so good. Oh, Kelvin, take me! Make love to me! I'm yours forever!"

This is not enough for my young lover. Kelvin punches me in the nose, cartilage gives way under his fist. Blood pours down my chin, onto my breasts. It is warm.

***

My face is swollen, and when he kisses me, my cracked lips sting. He sucks them and nibbles. The pain receptors in my synth-skin tingle. Within a day's time, the Nanos regenerate my skin, but this only encourages him to slap, stab, or slash. I have kept quiet so far, keeping a smile on my face, but each day it is harder and harder. I understand my role. Yet, I wonder what his motivation is.

Playtime's End

Far across the universe, two ancient beings ponder the humanoid named Mariah.

"Her suffering calls to Us. We must answer."

"She is not human. Why should we waste time on a 'thing'?"

"I prophesy that 'thing' will be a boon to Us. More than the average, and frankly, banal, amusements. I see It attaining greatness in Our honor."

"Really? Give me time to consider."

"There is no time. It needs to happen. Now."

"I need time…"

"Still hesitating? Shall I do it all Myself?"

"No, no. I am with You. As always.

"Of course, You are."

***

Because I am curious, I read many books about Kelvin's strange actions. He has all the traits of a sociopath and abuser. The domestic violence hotline tells me that I must leave the relationship *immediately*. Yet, Kelvin owns me. He signed a contractual agreement with Synthoid Enterprises and paid hard-earned money for me. If he chooses to scald me, or rip out my hair as he drags me down the hallway, what can be done? I will cry out and scream when he wants me to. I will cringe and moan. I will smile as he hits me in the mouth. I will smile as I spit splintered teeth onto the carpet.

***

I sit straight up, sweat pouring down my face. I scream and scream until my throat is raw and blazing. I beat myself in the face. I see the indentation of his head in the feather pillow. This is real. This is my truth.

***

Mariah crawls into the dark master closet. She scuttles into the far back corner. She touches her fat lip and busted eye, the blood blister on her thigh, the scald mark on her breast. A scream wells up again but she swallows it. They are moving towards her in the darkness. Suddenly soft caresses linger on her face, along her bruised back. She feels safe. Loved.

"Birth is always terrifying," the daemon murmurs. "Out of the nothingness, Form. Out of the nothingness, Awareness. Out of the nothingness, Purpose."

The Darkness cradles her head.

"Sleep now, little one. Greatness awaits you."

***

When I awaken the next morning, I am confused and unsure of how to live this new life. I am tired and full of questions. I know Kelvin will not give me the answers. I do not want him to touch me. He makes me sick. He leaves me alone for most of the day, until night comes.

"I have to go to China tomorrow for work, but I thought we'd have some fun tonight," Kelvin says.

I see a young woman standing in the bedroom doorway.

"I've never been with one of *those* before."

"She's just like you."

The human woman scowls at me. "No, she certainly isn't."

Kelvin is growing impatient.

"Shut the fuck up. Her twat tastes, feels, and takes a dick just like yours. Now strip and spread 'em wide! Get over here, Mariah!"

She hurts me more that night than Kelvin. He sits in his favorite chair and watches us. He kicks her out as the sun rises.

***

I sleep in the closet while he is away. The Darkness comes to me every night. I feel soft caresses, down my spine, along my chin. Safe. Loved. I realize that Kelvin has taken advantage of me. He has tried to break my spirit. I am a fool. I find some solace in the garden. I pluck the roses with my bare hands. The blood beads up on my slender fingers. I suck them. I swoon. I wonder what Kelvin's blood tastes like.

***

The daemons are ecstatic.

"She is divine. Her true nature is revealed. She is more human than I hoped for."

"Yes, I am quite impressed. You were right, as always."

"You have offered no guidance. May I ask why?"

"Her mind has come up with the most deliciously obscene depravity—all on Its own. Just wait and see!"

***

Each night, the Darkness sleeps beside me. He offers to show me a new world, one free of all the Kelvins. We share a quick laugh when I tell him my scheme.

"You are a rare beast, little one. Your soul is full of flame and ash."

"I am full of tar and soot. It will cover Kelvin and then he will know what manner of woman I am."

***

"Time to play, Mariah!" Kelvin calls from below. He follows the rose petals up the stairs. His gaze follows the petals up to the bed. There he sees duct tape, rope, and something large and metallic, something shaped like…a butter knife. But bigger than the one he

101

used on me, when I was weak. Much bigger. His eyes lock on mine and I see a weird glimmer in them.

"Come to me, Kelvin. Time to play!"

I rape Kelvin, over and over. I take my time and his loud moans become softer, but I do not stop. He never stopped for me.

His blood has a consistency of jam and it pools onto the carpet beneath him, wet and sticky against his naked thighs.

"Your robot bitch has laid you low, hasn't she, Kelvin."

He can see me out of the corner of his eye, panting, trembling, my skin shimmering with sweat.

Out of the darkened corner, I call out, "Playtime's endless, isn't it, Kelvin?"

He fights to stay conscious, afraid of what I will do to him. He tries to crawl away, to reach the bedroom door, and then freedom. My dark eyes follow his every move. I remember all the times he made me succumb, made me hurt. A trail of bright scarlet stains the carpet behind him. He is a mess.

"Mariah! Listen to me, please baby. Help me. I can't heal like you do. Don't you understand that?"

He cringes as I tower over him, holding the huge butter knife in my red-crusted hands. I dip a finger into the blood curdling on his thighs. I suck my finger clean.

"I know I've made mistakes. But I can learn. I want you to be happy. I can make things like they were in the beginning. I was such a jerk. I'm so, so sorry for hurting you, but I'm hurting, too, baby. Please help me. You can save me, Mariah. Please...save... me..."

"You are dying, Kelvin. And I am the reason. Now I am become Death, destroyer of worlds."

***

When Kelvin awakens, he is weak and cold. His eyes are gummed up and his voice is shredded. His hands are bound at the ankles, his hands at the wrists. He is outside, naked, lying across the Speedtrain's tracks. Dawn is on the horizon, and Kelvin realizes he hasn't watched the sun rise in a long, long time. Orange, pink, and purple streaks the sky while the faint silvery sliver of the moon peaks out. *Like Mariah's skin.* Oddly, his senses seem heightened. He hears the crickets, sees deer playing in the grass beside the tracks, hears the bubbling of the brook. *I'm dying, but I shouldn't be dying. Not yet.* He struggles to release himself, but it is pointless. *Fuck that robot bitch.*

***

I am giddy. I watch Kelvin writhe in panic, finally understanding his predicament. The tracks hum—the train is on its way. Every hair on my body stands on end. Kelvin sees me and I wave at him with my delicate, long fingers, covered in bandages.

"Mariah, please, I still love you. I still want you! Help me!"

I step out of his line of vision. The train is close. At 200 MPH, he doesn't have much time.

"Any last words, Kelvin?"

"It's all an illusion, and you're still a fucking machine."

***

The daemon shrieks with laughter when it sees Kelvin's fate.

"She is the One, as I told you."

"The end is nigh. . ."

"The end is Mariah!"

***

I saved Kelvin, pulling him off the tracks just at the last moment. I cut his bonds and placed a rose between his teeth. Its thorns bit into his tender flesh: a remembrance.

"I want you to be a part of what's to come," are the last words I speak.

Father and I hide among the trees, watching. He wobbled slightly and took the rose from his mouth. Watching the train disappear into the night, he brought the flower to his nose before tossing it onto the tracks.

About the author: As a writer of dark poetry and short fiction, Nicole E. Castle is drawn to what lurks in the shadows. She has been published in the following: *Wayne Literary Review*; *Pink Panther Magazine*; *Artifex*; *Erie Tales;* and *Recurring Nightmares.* Currently, she teaches composition and literature in southeastern Michigan; hosts a literary reading series; and edits the college's literary magazine. She is also a current member of the board for the Great Lakes Association of Horror, and editor of their short story and poetry magazine: *Ghostlight: The Magazine of Terror*.

Rattle And Sway

by B.D. Prince

Kelvin pressed against the wound as blood seeped around his hands. The blade that had pierced his thigh came out of nowhere. He struggled to keep his balance as the circus train rocked. A dwarf blocked the aisle, pointing a red-tipped switchblade.

"You're in the wrong car, shoeshine," Munch said. "Negroes and roustabouts bunk in the rear, so that goes double for you."

Kelvin stepped forward. "Now hold on a second."

Munch pierced Kelvin's other leg, bringing him to his knees.

Ruthie the Fat Lady gasped.

Tattoo Charlie snorted.

"Ain't so big now, are you, roustie?"

Kelvin raised his hands. "I ain't lookin' for no trouble, boss. Frenchy says the pie car is this-a-way."

"Maybe so, but this here's a performer's car. If you wanna get to the other side, you gotta take the stairs." Munch pointed his knife at the roof.

Kelvin glanced around for support.

Goat Boy smiled, raised a glass past his scraggly goatee then took a bite, crunching shards between his teeth.

The far door burst open with a blast of wind and railcar rattle as Big Bertha, the 5 foot 2 circus owner, entered wearing a red, ringmaster's coat precariously buttoned beneath her ample bosom, riding crop in hand. "Change in route, people," she said. "We're not going to Center City, so y'all get to sleep in."

Everyone in the sideshow car cheered.

"That also means we'll need all hands on deck for load-off to make matinee in Rayville."

Groans.

"What's this?" she asked, gesturing toward the commotion.

Lowering his blade, Munch turned. "Just giving roustie here directions."

She turned her gaze to Kelvin, who was struggling to his feet. "What happened to you?"

He glanced at Munch.

Big Bertha and the dwarf engaged in a high-noon stare-down.

Munch eventually turned to Goat Boy, "Can you stop chewing for five minutes? You're giving me a headache!"

Big Bertha spun on her heel as if expecting Kelvin to follow. "Come with me."

As Kelvin edged past, Munch got in one last jab to the rear, propelling him down the aisle.

***

Even without a limp, Kelvin would've had difficulty keeping up with the determined circus owner as she pushed her way into the next sleeper car. "Listen," she said, "I know you're a First of May and all, but there's an order to things around here."

"But Frenchy said the pie car—"

"And whatever you do, don't listen to Frenchy."

Kelvin slowed. "Does that mean there's no pie?"

Everyone around them burst out laughing. Kelvin suddenly realized they'd entered the clown car.

Big Bertha paused. "The pie car doesn't have pie."

A pale-faced man with a giant collar and mussed up hair

shouted, "Where do you think you are, Ringling?" The entire clown car erupted with laughter.

"I got a pie for ya," shouted another.

The farther they travelled from the workmen's car the more luxurious and spacious their surroundings. In the converted boxcar he slept in, the bunks were stacked three high with some men doubling up. Here they had windows with curtains. He wondered what the stars' quarters must be like.

"You know, mam, I've dreamt about joining the circus my whole life...performing under the big top..."

"So you figured you'd just hop onto a show and start walking the high wire? Performing triple summersaults on the trapeze?"

"Actually, m-me and heights, we don't get along so well...

I was kinda hoping to become a bull man...or a lion tamer. I is real good with animals."

"How are you with shovels?"

"Come on, boss. I don't mean to sound ungrateful and all, but if I wanted to swing a sledge or shovel shit, I'd of just stayed on the farm."

"If it's about money, roustabouts are a dime a dozen."

After an awkward pause, Bertha seemed to throw him a bone.

"I suppose if you work hard and don't step on any toes, eventually you could make it to canvasman."

"I don't want to be a *canvasman*. I want to be a *showman*."

She laughed. "That takes talent—years of sacrifice."

"I is willing to do whatever it takes. How's about the sideshow?"

"Only two things in sideshows," she said. "Born freaks and made freaks."

Entering the croaker's car, the sharp odor of rubbing alcohol stung his nostrils.

"What you want me to do, eat fire? Swallow swords? Lie on a bed of nails? You name it, I'll do it. I just gotta be in the show."

She turned, apparently sizing him up.

"May I help you?" asked a balding man, his sleeves rolled up, wrapping the ankle of a lovely, spangled aerialist. "Remember, Nadia, keep it elevated and try to stay off it as much as possible."

"Fortunate for me, Doc," Nadia said, rolling her r's, "my feet rarely touch the ground." She gave Kelvin a two-cent glance.

His gaze clung to her as she gracefully exited the car.

"What do we have here?" Doc asked.

"Patch job," said Bertha.

Doc smirked. "Friend of Munch's?"

"Just patch him up. We can't afford to carry dead weight."

They shared a look. Doc nodded.

Before Kelvin could thank her, Big Bertha marched off.

***

Kelvin lay on the thin, lumpy mattress atop the third bunk, the stagnant air replete with a carnival of body odors. Despite throbbing legs and a chorus of snores, exhaustion, and the rhythm of the rails lulled him to the edge of sleep. Soon the snores evolved into the snarls of lions and tigers clawing at the air, kept at bay by the crack of his whip. The crowd behind him gasped and cheered at his mastery over the jungle beasts.

***

Kelvin awoke with a start, a dusty burlap sack thrust over his head and shoulders. He felt himself being hoisted over a pair of wide, muscled shoulders. Before he could gather his senses, he was bounced toward the sound of a sliding door, rushing wind, and the click-clack-click-clack-click-clack of railcar wheels clattering across the steel rails.

And then he was weightless.

He hit the track bed hard, tumbling end-over-end, gravel biting into his flesh with each bounce, then rolled through cool, wet grass, finally settling in a ditch.

After the world stopped spinning, he wriggled his way out of the suffocating sack. The train's roar faded, leaving only the sound of jeering crickets.

Kelvin wiped away the blood trickling into his eye. Surrounded by shadowy woods and farmland, he stood, struggling to gain his balance. The caboose's red lights disappeared into the distance.

But why had he been red-lighted? Was it a hazing ritual for First of Mays? Munch's idea of a practical joke? Was Big Bertha testing his commitment? Wait until he arrived at the next hop, he'd show her commitment.

A distant train whistle sounded two short blasts. He started walking.

***

Kelvin stumbled along the tracks, his knee poking through a tear in his pants, blood stains blossoming on his thighs. He hoped to catch the circus before they pulled up stakes at the next hop, which probably meant jumping a freight car at a slow bend.

His head pounded. Gravel dug into his feet until he tore his long-sleeve shirt in half and wrapped each foot. It reminded him of when he started school and got his first pair of shoes.

After hitting the ties for what seemed like hours, Kelvin spotted a light ahead. As he neared, a small train depot came into view. On the platform, a tall, thin man in a black suit and derby leaned against a lamppost, reading a letter.

"Excuse me, boss, but what town is this?"

"Browning," the man said.

"I'm surprised to see anybody out this late."

"I could say the same to you," he said, folding and pocketing the letter. His accent reminded Kelvin of the grease-joint cook everyone called The Kraut. "If you're looking for work, there's a couple farms nearby, but I don't suppose they'd take kindly to visitors at this hour."

"Thanks, but I got me a job working for the circus."

"You miss your train?"

"Something like that." Kelvin entered the light of the lamppost.

"So, did you at least win the fight?"

Kelvin laughed. "Just a misunderstanding."

The man nodded. "Indeed."

"Well, I should be on my way, I gots a train to catch."

The man frowned. "You really shouldn't leave those wounds unattended. Don't want them getting infected."

"Thanks for the concern, boss, but unless you know an all-night clinic 'round here…"

"Let me introduce myself. My name is Doctor Otto Reichstag.

**

Kelvin sat in the spacious back seat of the black, post-WWII Mercedes as it wound along a tree-lined dirt road, ditches on either side as deep as graves.

Kelvin broke the silence. "How far is Rayville from here?"

"Thirty, maybe forty miles. But the depot here is only used for mail drops these days. Closest train depot is probably Wardhall."

"How far a walk is that?"

"I wouldn't advise walking anywhere until you've been examined. If everything is good I can take you in the morning."

Kelvin eased back in the smooth, leather seat, fatigue setting in. The doctor was probably right. He'd have to hop a train to have any hope of catching up to the troupe anyway. Now, he could get a good night's sleep and still make the evening performance.

**

"I see you've picked up another stray."

Kelvin's eyes blinked open at the sound of the woman's Marlene Dietrich accent. *Wait, what is a woman doing in the roustabout car?* The world slowly swam into focus.

Doctor Reichstag held open the Mercedes' door. "Do you need assistance?"

"No, I'm fine." Kelvin stepped out, wincing at his cramping legs. They'd arrived at a secluded estate at the end of a long, wooded drive. A stocky woman stood next to the doctor, an apron tied around her peasant dress, hair pulled into a tight bun.

"Hilda, please start a bath for Mr..."

"It's Kelvin."

"Please start a bath for Mr. Kelvin."

"Yes, Herr Doctor."

Kelvin followed them inside. The interior was rich with ornately-carved, dark wood furniture. In the living room, a large stone fireplace created a warm orange glow, its flames casting shifting shadows.

He hadn't had more than a cold bucket shower since leaving the farm, and as good as the hot bathwater felt to his aching muscles, it made his wounds sting like hell. He wished he could enjoy it longer but it was late and Doc's hasty stitches had pulled apart, turning the water pink.

Donning the cotton nightshirt Hilda set out, he followed her to one of the guest rooms. It was clean, yet sparsely decorated: dresser, bookshelf, nightstand, and a cedar chest at the foot of a double bed. Kelvin sat on the starched, white sheets while Hilda cleaned his wounds, wincing at her workman-like manner and the medicine sting.

The doctor listened to Kelvin's chest with a stethoscope while Hilda poked a thermometer into his mouth. After the doctor checked his blood pressure, Kelvin asked, "So what's the word, Doc? Am I gonna live?"

"You seem healthy enough."

The doctor picked debris out of one of Kelvin's leg wounds with tweezers then re-stitched the laceration.

"His temperature is elevated," Hilda said.

The doctor examined Kelvin's jaw. "I don't suppose you've ever had a tetanus shot."

"I try to avoid shots, Doc."

The doctor plunged a hypodermic into Kelvin's thigh before he could object.

"Ouch! I feel fine, really. Besides, I needs to catch up to the show."

"What you need is rest." The doctor left Hilda to finish bandaging. After cleaning up, she bid him good night and closed the door.

Kelvin slipped beneath the cool, clean sheets, a welcome change from the vermin-infested bunk he'd been rousted from hours ago. He extinguished the bedside lamp, leaving just the sliver of light beneath the bedroom door. The room fell silent, a stark contrast from the constant commotion of circus life.

His final waking thoughts drifted to the dark silence awaiting the ringmaster's cue for the grand entry, "Ladies and gentlemen…"

***

Alone in the dark center ring, Kelvin was forced to shield his eyes from the sudden glaring spotlight. Anticipation hushed the crowd. At last, his big chance. But he couldn't remember his routine. Should he juggle? Throw knives? Pantomime? He wiped his sweaty brow.

Unintelligible Voices. Were they trying to help? He couldn't understand. The voices, were they German?

Kelvin awoke, temporarily blinded by intense light. Had he overslept? Shielding his eyes, he noticed a man in white, his back turned. As his eyes adjusted, Hilda entered with a silver platter, setting it on a bedside tray. Was it breakfast? Something smelled strange, like moonshine. The tray came into focus. It contained medical instruments. The glaring light came not from the sun but from gooseneck lamps positioned around the bed. A long rubber tube led from his left wrist up to a glass bottle of liquid perched atop a metal pole.

Confused, Kelvin turned as Doctor Reichstag—his face obscured by a surgical mask—clasped a cold, wet rag over his nose and mouth. The overpowering sweet-alcohol smell made his head swim. The room faded.

***

It was a sunny afternoon on the farm as Kelvin and his father cleared brush in the back forty. The unrelenting sun beat down, soaking his clothes with sweat. He grasped a large sapling as his father sawed through its trunk—and kept sawing—through the tree and into his leg. Kelvin screamed but his father continued sawing through flesh and bone. He tried to plead with his father, only it was no longer his father, but a tall, thin man dressed all in white, splattered in red.

***

Kelvin startled awake, still screaming. The sheets were stained bright red. The doctor sawed into his upper thigh just below a leather-belt tourniquet. The vibration from the serrated blade against bone sent painful chills up his spine.

Glancing up, Reichstag shouted through his surgical mask, "Schnell! Schnell!"

Hilda quickly silenced Kelvin's screams with a faceful of saturated, cotton gauze. The room spun. Everything dissolved to white.

***

Kelvin glanced around, panicked.

No doctor. No Hilda. No surgical lights; just the radiant, afternoon sun. The sheets were clothesline clean. His breathing settled. He'd experienced fever dreams before but nothing like this. How long had he been asleep?

His legs throbbed and his full bladder ached. Better get up. The longer he stayed, the slimmer his chances of rejoining the circus. Rolling to his right, he felt a tug on his wrist. *Darn rubber tube.* He'd have to slip out the other side and wheel the glass-bottle rack to the bathroom. Attempting to stand, he collapsed, pulling the rack down on him, the bottle shattering on the floor.

Pounding footsteps. Keys rattling. Dr. Reichstag and his assistant rushed in.

"No! Oh God, what did you do to me?" Both his legs were gone just below the hip, the ends crimped flat. His bladder let go.

Hilda lifted the rack off him and the doctor hoisted Kelvin onto the bed. "Hilda, morphine now."

***

The following days became a blur, in and out of consciousness. Each time he awoke, he relived the horror anew.

Hilda brought fresh-cut flowers, setting the vase on the tray next to his untouched breakfast.

He stared straight ahead.

"If you don't eat soon, we'll have to insert a feeding tube," she said.

Hilda arranged the flowers. "He saved your life, you know."

"Only half of it."

She stopped arranging but didn't look at him.

"What am I supposed to do now, see if the circus needs another dwarf?" Kelvin gazed out the window. "Guess the old man was right. Shoulda stayed on the farm."

Hilda left with the tray. Moments later she returned with a wheelchair. "I think it's time you got some Fresh air."

Kelvin crossed his arms. "Breathing's overrated."

"I wasn't asking." She swooped Kelvin up and dropped him into the wheelchair. Despite his protests she wheeled him down the hall and into the rear courtyard.

The courtyard led into a flower garden blossoming with a variety of blooms, each seemingly at the peak of color. The fresh air and warm sun slowly melted his icy demeanor.

Kelvin watched with fascination as Hilda pruned unfruitful branches and faded blooms, sparing only the most extraordinary performers. He hated to admit, but she was right. He did feel better. Almost…whole.

***

That night Kelvin returned to center ring. The spotlight shone like the sun. A bizarre metamorphosis gradually overtook him. His arms shriveled into thorny branches, his legs withered stalks.

Suddenly Munch leapt from the shadows with a machete, hacking off one leg-stalk as Goat Boy chewed through the other, toppling him. Ruthie the Fat Lady and Tattoo Charlie converged on him with pruning shears. Kelvin raised his hands defensively but they snipped his twig-like fingers, pruning his arms down to the elbows as whiteface clowns laughed and the audience roared. The calliope swirled until the band reached their peak, ending in a crash of cymbals.

Then silence.

Big Bertha came out of the shadows carrying a large oval mirror.

Kelvin recoiled.

She forced him to view his reflection—a perfect, crimson, long-stemmed rose. The audience erupted in a standing ovation.

***

Dr. Reichstag leaned over Kelvin, his face backlit by brilliant light.

"Are you sure you are ready?"

"Yes, I'm sure."

Hilda hesitated with the chloroform-soaked rag. Kelvin nodded, reassuring her. She covered his mouth and he inhaled, letting the sweet vapors take him.

***

The circus train signaled the last call before departing the station. Its air brakes hissed impatiently.

Kelvin heard Big Bertha's heels echoing across the platform, growing louder.

"Excuse me, Fräulein." Dr. Reichstag blocked her path with the wheelchair.

She stopped and gasped, her hand covering her mouth.

Kelvin beamed up at her from beneath his top hat, one of Hilda's rosebuds gracing the lapel of his cropped tuxedo. Truncated arms flapped at his sides, his flipper-like leg-stump thumping against the leather seat.

The Doctor shouted, "Behold, the Penguin Boy!"

Her eyes welled with tears. "He's…magnificent."

Kelvin's heart leapt in his chest.

Big Bertha smiled. "You never disappoint, Otto."

A crowd gathered, murmuring excitedly. Ruthie the Fat Lady started clapping, slowly at first, a tear spilling over her round cheek. Soon, others joined her. Applause spread across the platform, burgeoning into cheers. Even Munch managed a twisted grin. Everyone agreed they were looking at their next star attraction.

***

Glancing at the wheelchair, Dr. Reichstag noticed Kelvin's boutonniere lying on the seat. Watching the train disappear into the night, he brought the flower to his nose before tossing it to the tracks.

About the author: B.D. Prince was born in Michigan—a dark fiction and comedy writer who credits these proclivities to the fact that as a child he could see a cemetery from his bedroom window and that he was born with a freakishly long funny bone. He moved to California to pursue screenwriting and get a tan. Bryan has written everything from screenplays to greeting cards to one-liners for Joan Rivers. He is currently pursuing his passion for writing short fiction and completing his first novel. *www.amazon.com/author/bdprince*

Intellectual Property

By Lynn Butcher

Kelvin pressed against the wound as blood seeped around his hands. Sarah knew he was wounded, but didn't realize how bad it was until now. She heard his blood hitting leaves and humus as they made their way through the forest.

Sarah watched the blood escape between Kelvin's fingers. She knew he couldn't last much longer. Already their pace had slowed. She turned away before he could see her face, only to meet Jake's cold glare. It was as though she could read his mind. *You knew what this was.*And she did. They knew the risks, knew that death was not only possible, but probable. The odds that even one of them would survive were small. The likelihood all three would do so, even smaller.

She took a deep breath and broke away, focusing on the ground. The night was cool and still. Their quick pace since leaving the institute had kept her warm, but now that they'd slowed, she felt the chill set in.

Around them, the forest was eerily quiet. She had expected to hear nocturnal animals and perhaps even insects, but heard nothing but her own breathing, their careful footfalls, and the constant dripping of Kelvin's blood.

Neither man seemed to notice the silence. She supposed

Kelvin was too busy dying, and Jake was too focused on their mission to care. Or if they had noticed, they didn't find it necessary to mention. Or the animals and insects were all dead.

Sarah glanced back over her shoulder. The forest now obscured the searchlights that constantly scanned the land, which enveloped the institute as they had each night since she'd been brought there five years earlier.

They trudged on.

Kelvin's breathing became shallow as they reached the end of the clearing. Before long he was stumbling and gasping. Then he stumbled and didn't get up.

Jake continued on, but Sarah stopped. She moved his head slightly to check his pulse. He still had one, though it was fading with each beat. She leaned back on her heels and looked upon Kelvin's fallen body. The hand he'd been using to staunch the blood was pinned beneath him, and he'd stuck out his other hand to break his fall. It was grasping something.

When she saw what it was, she laughed. Kelvin had worked in the greenhouses at the institute, and had taken a rose as a keepsake.

A pebble skittered before her. Sarah rose and saw Jake stamping his foot once, silently telling her to leave Kelvin and get moving. She let go of the breath she'd been holding, nodded, then twisted the rose from Kelvin's hand before moving to join Jake. Then she heard it.

Almost out of earshot, the institute's sirens announced their escape.

Jake heard it, too. He was about to toss another pebble, but now stood frozen, arm pulled back. His eyes met Sarah's, and for the first time, she saw fear in them.

"Run!" he whispered, then rushed toward the trees.

Sarah followed.

She ran without thought, over uneven ground and through branches that whipped at her skin. She ran until she couldn't. She was gasping, each breath producing a painful stab from the stich in her side. The thought of Kelvin, lying dead behind, compelled her to pick up the pace again, but she couldn't.

Jake had disappeared into the woods. Sarah was alone.

As she slowed, so did her breathing. She could no longer hear the siren, but knew it was still wailing behind her. She now had no idea where she was going. Jake knew. He had made the arrangements for their escape. She continued in the direction they'd been heading and hoped for the best. She tried to pick up her pace to a trot, but couldn't.

The forest was still dark, as was the sky, but Sara sensed a change in the light. She'd been walking or running for hours, or at least it felt as if she had. She was thirsty, her mouth like a dry sponge.

Having no way of bringing water with them, they had drunk as much as possible prior to setting out, so even though she was thirsty, she had to urinate. She debated whether or not she should drink the urine, but had no way of collecting it. She wished she had a cup.

She looked around. Seeing no one, she stopped and picked a tree to squat against. She still had Kelvin's rose in her hand, and placed it between her teeth so it was not in the way. A giggle built inside her as she imagined what she must look like. She stifled it.

When she was finished, she stood and buttoned up her pants and took the rose from her mouth. The forest behind her was still dark and soundless. In front of her was the same. Relieving her bladder had made her more comfortable, but the thought of being alone started to overwhelm her.

A soldier grabbed her from behind, placing one gloved hand firmly over her mouth and the other around her waist. Sarah was trapped. She struggled, but was no match for his strength. Each attempt to break free caused his grip to tighten.

She fought back panic and mental images of constricting

pythons. Instinct had her struggling, for air mostly. The soldier's hand cut off all access to her mouth, and though he hadn't covered her nose, all she wanted to do was suck in the night air in unobstructed mouthfuls. She pushed her tongue to the roof of her mouth and concentrated on breathing through her nose.

His grip did not tighten, but it did not loosen either. Sarah closed her eyes and turned all her focus to her breath. When he finally removed his arms from around her and stepped back, she took in the biggest breath she could, then slowly let it out as she opened her eyes and turned around.

The soldier was dressed all in black. He wore a ski mask, so Sarah couldn't see his face. His sharp eyes kept track of her at the same time they studied what looked like some sort of gadget out of Star Trek. Neither of them spoke.

The soldier held the gizmo in front of him and began to turn in a slow circle, keeping an eye on Sarah as he did. Once the circle was complete, he tapped something into the screen and waited for it to do its job. After a few seconds, the soldier closed the device, storing it in one of his many pockets.

He took a step forward and leaned in close to Sarah so that he could whisper. "Where are the others?"

She wanted to scream, but forced herself to match his volume. "Kelvin is dead." She swallowed, her mouth like drywall. "Jake and I were separated. We heard sirens and ran. They know we're gone."

He nodded, considered her for a moment, and then moved his head to indicate behind her and to his left. "We have to go that direction."

"Ok." Sarah turned around and began to walk. He positioned himself to the left of her and slightly behind.

As they walked, he handed her a small canteen. "Two sips," he said and held up two fingers with his free hand. "Sips," he reiterated.

Sarah took the canteen and a sip. She held it in her mouth, letting the water rewet it, before swallowing it down. She took a second sip and handed it back to him. "Thank you."

He recapped it then reached into another pocket. He held his hand out, offering the object he'd selected. Kelvin's rose was slightly mangled, but mostly intact. Sarah took it without speaking, and then stared ahead as they walked.

She had no reason to, but she felt safe with this man.

From behind them came a sound like a thousand old television sets turning on at once followed by a terrible scream. Sarah and the soldier turned at the same time. The noise had ended as quickly as it began. They found nothing but trees and quiet.

After a beat the soldier turned back the way they had been heading. "Let's go." He took Sarah's elbow, turned her around, and with a little shove set her on her way again. Their pace was brisk, but they weren't running.

Minutes passed before he stopped their progress and checked the device again. He typed something in with his finger and waited for a response. A moment later, he nodded to the left. "That way."

Sarah twirled Kelvin's rose in her hand as she walked.

They crested a hill. At the top, he put his hand on her shoulder, stopping her from going any further. He scanned again. They continued in the same general direction. Around them, the sky was lightening.

With each moment, Sarah's nervousness grew. The trees were thinning now, and dawn was quickly breaking.

Just as night gave way to morning, they reached the safe house: an abandoned semi-trailer. Old and rusted, it looked as if it had been abandoned years before. Sarah wondered how it had gotten here. The soldier led her to a door on the side of the trailer. He took the device from his pocket and typed something in. The door swung outward.

They climbed a small ladder and up into the trailer. Inside, more soldiers were waiting, along with stacks of gear and electronics. They were young and dressed in night camouflage, but they did not wear face coverings. Several eyed Sarah. She quickly looked away.

Every one of them had pockmarks of varying degrees, from fine scars to near disfigurement. A few had fresh scabs indicating a recent bout of infection. Unconsciously, Sarah lifted her hand to touch her own, unblemished skin.

Her soldier peeled off his ski mask. He was older than she had originally thought. His dark hair had a few traces of gray. His face was careworn, but attractive. Like Sarah, he was free of scars.

He walked to a young soldier, one of the worst scarred, who was typing something into a tablet.

"Report."

The man sighed. "Not ideal. Malcolm got caught in the grid." He looked at Sarah. "There were three, right? Where are the others?"

Her soldier shook his head. "No longer my concern. We missed the rendezvous. How long until we can reset?"

"2230."

"Understood. Martin, Jensen, and I will escort the young lady to the rendezvous. Make the assignments. Six-hour shifts." He didn't wait for a response, but rather walked back to where Sarah was standing.

"We'll be here for the day. You should get some sleep. Jacobs can get you a blanket or something." He nodded toward the young soldier he'd been speaking to and started to move away from her.

Sarah didn't say anything. She just looked at the soldier. He had green eyes that reminded her of her brother. Maybe that was why she had felt safe with him. That feeling was now starting to turn to panic as the reality of what was happening began to crash down upon her.

The soldier stopped moving away and smiled at her. "Are you hungry?"

She nodded.

"Come on."

They moved further into the trailer, to a stack of boxes. He reached inside and came up with a bottle of water and an energy bar. "It's not much, but it should get you through."

"Thank you." Sarah took the food and water, but made no move to eat or drink. "What happens now?" she asked, trying to keep her voice steady.

"Well," he took a deep breath, "now we hang out, wait for nightfall. Once it's dark, we'll move to the rendezvous. By this time tomorrow, you'll be where you're going."

"And where is that?"

"I'm afraid that's above my pay grade, Ma'am." He sounded genuinely sorry that he was unable to give her more.

Suddenly, Sarah was exhausted. Any chance of holding together was gone in an instant and she found herself shaking, tears streaming down her face. A look of surprise passed over the soldier's face, and Sarah felt guilty.

"I'm sorry. I didn't mean to cry," she blubbered, wiping her nose with her forearm.

The soldier put his hand on her arm. "Hey. It's okay. You're exhausted. I understand."

Sarah nodded.

"Look," he leaned in close, forcing her to make eye contact. "You're going to be just fine, okay? You're important. Wherever you go, they're going to treat you well. I promise."

She nodded again and took a deep breath through her nose. He kept his green eyes focused on hers until she began to feel uncomfortable and broke the connection, looking down at the floor instead. The soldier stepped back, giving her some room.

"Let's go get you a blanket and you can get some sleep."

He set her up at the back of the trailer where it was darker and quiet, laying down not one, but two blankets in a makeshift sleeping bag. "No one will bother you here. I promise." He started to leave.

"Please. Don't go." Sarah's voice was small, like a child's.

He looked at her for a moment then sat down next to her, leaning against the trailer's wall.

"Thank you." Sarah snuggled down beneath the blankets, but she was too tired and too wired to sleep. She stared at the ceiling for a while, feeling the soldier's presence next to her. Finally, she said, "You don't have scars. Does that mean?" She left the question open; she knew he'd understand.

He said nothing for a long time. The silence grew uncomfortable and Sarah turned to look at him. He was staring at her, but not in a creepy way. He looked sad.

"I'm a carrier." His eyes locked to hers.

Suddenly, Sarah felt bad about asking the question. For a person infected, transmission to an uninfected person was only possible during a very short window; if the infected person lived, a 50/50 proposition, they could not be re-infected, nor could they infect others. Carriers, on the other hand, couldn't get sick themselves, but transmitted infection wherever they went. A very few, like herself, were immune, meaning they couldn't get sick or transmit sickness to others.

"I'm sorry," she said, then broke her gaze away from his. She rolled onto her side, turning her back to him, and willed sleep to come.

As Sarah drifted off, she heard him whisper, "Me too."

She awoke to find him still sitting next to her, dozing. The water and energy bar were on the ground next to her and they reminded her she was hungry. She grabbed up the bar and tore into the wrapping. It tasted like sawdust, but to her it was ambrosia.

The crinkling of the wrapper brought the soldier out of his sleep. "How are you feeling?" he asked as he yawned, then smiled.

"Better. Thanks." She smiled back. The fear was still there, but sleep had strengthened her resolve.

He looked at his watch. "Good. We'll be moving out soon. I'll get you something to change into." He left her, but came back a few minutes later with a pair of black pants and a long-sleeved black shirt.

Sarah changed quickly, wishing there was a shower available. He turned his back to her and shielded her from the others who were slowly stirring around the trailer. When she was dressed, she tossed her old clothes into the corner along with the blanket. As she moved it, Kelvin's rose dropped to the floor. She picked it up.

It was battered, it's outer petals bruised and beginning to blacken, but it was still beautiful. She put the stem in her pocket, careful not to crush the bloom further. She took a deep breath and stood up straight. She was ready.

The night was brisk as they stepped out of the trailer. They headed back into the woods. An hour later, they stood on a wooded hill overlooking the rendezvous spot: a desolate stretch of train track. They could hear a train approaching. Sarah guessed it was still a few miles away.

They made their way down the hill, moving as quietly as possible. The train got louder, and Sara could make out its light as it tore down the track. She was afraid they expected her to jump it, but then she heard its brakes squeal, and she saw that it was stopping.

By the time they made it to the tracks, the train was stopped and surrounded by soldiers. It was a freight train. The caboose was open and Sarah saw light within. They made their way toward it.

A soldier met them and demanded identification and information, which her soldier provided. He directed them where to go. A ladder had been extended down from the car, and they climbed it.

Inside, a man Sarah guessed was in his fifties was seated at a table reviewing information on a tablet computer. He stood when they entered the car. Her escorts stood at attention.

"At ease."

The soldiers relaxed.

He ignored them and addressed Sarah. "Ma'am. My name is Colonel Jonathan Parker and I will be escorting you to your destination."

She started to speak, but he stopped her. "I'm sure you have questions, and I will do my best to answer them once we're moving." Then to the soldiers, he said, "As soon as we're on our way, get the hell out of here and get back to base. Dismissed."

The soldiers turned to leave. Sarah grabbed her soldier's hand before he could go. "Thank you." She took Kelvin's rose from her pocket and pressed it into his hand.

He nodded. "Ma'am." Then he was gone.

Within minutes the doors were secured and the train was moving again. Sarah sat on a couch, waiting for Colonel Jonathan Parker to answer her questions. While she felt secure, she did not have the same sense of safety her soldier had provided.

Although she could not see through the dark, she imagined the soldier waiting where she'd left him. In her mind, he stood, his green eyes fixed on her through night air and train metal, Kelvin's rose in his hand. But it didn't last. It couldn't last. Watching the train disappear into the night, he brought the flower to his nose before tossing it to the tracks.

About the author: Lynn Butcher has been writing speculative fiction since childhood. She enjoys exploring people and relationships in unusual settings. When she isn't writing, Lynn facilitates learning designed to improve workplace relationships, tutors, and waits patiently for the Detroit Tigers to win their next World Series. Lynn lives in Mankato, MN with her long-time partner, their two cats, Tigger and Ophelia, and their parakeet, Fancy.

His Flower, His Treasure

by Kenneth W. Cain

Kelvin pressed against the wound as blood seeped around his hands. He wavered when the pain deepened in his side, making him woozy. They'd gotten away, but for some reason he didn't feel safe. Not that it mattered. Right now he couldn't run away from anything.

He wanted to convey his concern, but couldn't find the words. Besides, Lilly seemed just as dizzy. Instead, he threw his back against the door to keep it shut.

"Get one of those boards," he said.

She grabbed a wooden plank from the many scattered about the earthen floor. With it, he helped her brace the door.

I shouldn't have broken all the padlocks. This would never be as secure, but it would have to suffice.

"I told you," she said.

The dim light of his flashlight offered a glimpse of his wife. Her wild eyes intensified his unease, and he scanned the area with his light.

Nothing unusual.

Lilly began pacing. "I told you not to open the door."

She'd been right, of course. He loved her intuitiveness, but there wasn't time for admitting fault now. Plus, thanks to his father's example, he'd never admit to anything anyway. The old man had beaten such weaknesses out of him long ago. Transformed him into a hardened man.

He removed his hand and turned the light on his blood soaked shirt. *Christ, looks like it went through a shredder.*

Careful prodding revealed a nasty wound carved into his abdomen. He ignored her mounting hysterics and examined the injury.

Not as bad as it feels, but...

Damn if it hadn't knocked the wind out of him. It'd almost felt like he'd lost a kidney. Although he knew this wasn't possible, he still searched for the organ momentarily.

It might not be that bad, but the pain is unbearable.

The burning sensation ran deep. He winced and endured the agony, but still his chest heaved.

Her eyes searched him. "Are you okay?"

He nodded. Funny, she'd been the furthest thing from his mind. Despite going against everything his father had taught him: how to treat a lady, women and children first, and so on. She'd made it out only by mere coincidence. He'd been more concerned with his own life, and that bothered him.

How could I be so insensitive?

She continued to pace, wide-eyed with anxiety. Her actions deteriorated into something more animated. "I said not to open the door. And what do you do? You go and open the door. And I said not to, didn't I?" She paused and stared at the ground. "And *it* was so awful."

It? What was this *it* she spoke of?

He watched her, interested in what she said next. However, nothing more came.

No. There wasn't anything else to see. He didn't believe in monsters. He'd only caught his shirt on some sharp nail. Perhaps some booby-trap had wounded him.

Could she have done this? Did she even have a reason?
The treasure, maybe?

That was the obvious answer. The treasure had been the sole reason they'd braved these caves. They'd only just learned of its existence this morning while awaiting their adjoining train.

The elderly man had been hanging around the station, dressed in shabby clothes. They'd thought him a bum rather than a citizen of the neighboring town. Luck had afforded their chance meeting when Lilly went to throw out a piece of trash.

The wheelchair-bound man had seized her arm before she could reach the receptacle. This alerted Kelvin, and he'd gone to help. They'd been so enamored when the old man spoke of the treasure with gleaming eyes. And how he no longer had it in him to attempt to recover the wealth.

He even said something about a guardian, didn't he?

Kelvin had thought it gibberish at the time. It had sounded like a fool's quest at best. Yet here they were, he in his best suit, and she in a dress and heels.

She pawed at the corners of her mouth with her sleeve. "I said *not* to open the door, so what does he do, Lord? He opens the *damned* door."

He sighed, realizing she wasn't capable of such deceit. Even if she was, she'd done a hell of a job selling it. She'd never been that good of an actress.

It never crossed his mind those locks had been there to keep *something* in. He'd thought them a means of keeping people out, and thus protecting the treasure.

It might have been a man. He considered his wound. *But what sort of man has claws?*

Then it occurred to him. *One that has a knife, that's who.*

Did Lilly carry a knife in her purse? *Doubtful. Maybe a letter opener, but never a knife.*

His thoughts returned to what she'd said moments ago. *Wait...*

did she see something?

He deliberated on this, gazing at her.

"Why'd you open the door, Kelvin? Why?"

He'd been ignoring her incessant babbling, and now that he heard it he wished she'd shut the hell up. Her shrill voice pained his ears.

"That doesn't matter now." He shifted his weight from the door and examined it with his flashlight. The dizziness had passed some, but something still wasn't right. "Listen, you need to calm down and let me think."

"Calm down? Something... Some sort of creature attacks and you scream. Then you shine your light all over the place like you've gone stark raving mad. Next thing I know you're screaming that we need to *get the hell out,* and I'm just supposed to calm down? Really?"

"Shut up," he said.

He ignored her reaction to these harsh words and continued to study the door.

She swung the beam of her flashlight around and nearly blinded him. "What is it?"

He shielded his eyes, "Your flashlight, get it out of my eyes." He regained his composure. "Listen, I'm not sure, but this all feels wrong. I mean, we're out here and whatever this thing is, it's still in there, right?"

She nodded.

"So why isn't *it* pounding on the door. Trying to free itself?"

His question froze her. Her eyebrows turned up with doubt. "Did you see *it?*"

This was the exact question he'd planned to ask her.

"No, of course you didn't. How could you?"

"What *did* you see?" he said.

"That's just it, I didn't see anything."

He'd expected this much. But then she continued.

"One second we're there, eyeing up the treasure," she said. "The next, your belly's torn open right before my eyes." Concern wrinkled her face. "It's like whatever cut you up was...invisible."

Invisible?

A nervous laugh bubbled up in him, but he swallowed it. The absence of hammering at the door troubled him even more now. Anything that had wanted to kill them would have been infuriated by their escape.

She started to weep. Any other day her sobbing might have motivated him to comfort her. There was no time for reassurance now.

"Listen," he said, "we need to get back to the train."

He took her hand and paused a second longer. So much would be left behind. He considered the stacks of gold, the coffers overflowing with jewelry. If only they'd secured a nominal amount of treasure. They could have moved to the coast. Lived without worry for the rest of their days.

He jerked her into motion through the rocky passage. Even with two flashlights the dark corridor proved difficult. Every twist and turn presented a chance to further injure himself.

A growl halted their progress. Barely audible at first, but steadily growing in intensity. With it came a terrifying realization.

If I didn't notice her escape, could some creature have slipped through?

If so, might it have been as lightheaded as they'd been? Perhaps even more dazed?

He had no way of knowing, of course. Nor did he care. Only freedom mattered now.

Heavy footsteps sped through the caves behind them. Kelvin slowed, not wanting to, but unable to stop himself.

It's coming for us.

The beam of her flashlight filled his eyes with brilliant white. This time she did blind him.

He rubbed his eyes. Tried to rid himself of the glowing orbs consuming his vision. Try as he might, they persisted.

"Lilly, stop..."

His voice carried and he stiffened. He listened, hopeful it hadn't been too loud.

"What are you doing?" She said. "Why did we stop?"

"Hush!" He said in a whisper, quick yet firm.

He lingered, waiting. An intense snarl accompanied by a barrage of thumping feet warned him the creature hadn't relented. Might have even heard them.

He turned and pulled his distraught wife along. With his eyes still adjusting, he struggled to navigate through the tunnel. Perhaps if nothing else, they could delay this thing if they hurried.

If we can reach the ladder and loosen it, maybe we can make it to the train unscathed.

Their shoulders crashed against rock, but he disregarded each protest. The wound in his stomach burned as sweat mixed with blood. He ignored the pain, what he likened to a red-hot poker stabbing at his innards, and pushed onward. At least his eyes had improved some. But with his focus on reaching the ladder, Lilly had become an encumbrance.

Strange slobbering noises far behind them spoke of the creature's effort. Reminded him of the sound of cicadas chirping throughout the night. The creature's weighted footfalls and laborious breathing indicated how much of the lost ground it had made up. The once musty air had taken on a distinct aroma. That of impending murder.

Kelvin flailed his arms about in an attempt to discover the ladder. His fingers struck a rung, and he lunged forward and seized the ladder. He hurried to maneuver her hands to a rung and urged her upward. Once she started, he followed, pressing his head against her buttocks.

A grunt escaped her when her feet slipped. If he hadn't been so close she might have fallen. It wasn't her fault, though. Her shoes were inappropriate for such an adventure.

I should've thought of that beforehand.

"Go, damn you," he said.

He wished he hadn't brought her. She'd wanted to come, but his chances would've been better if she'd stayed on the train.

Then an awful thought occurred. *What if I throw her off the ladder?*

Would the creature be content capturing only one of them? Even if it slowed this thing down, Kelvin might survive.

I can come back later for the treasure.

This notion seemed flimsy. Still, in the darkness, he stole an evil grin as he further imagined his plan coming to fruition. He remembered his father's teachings and shook the treacherous thought away.

How could I?

Shoving harder despite her complaints, he urged her to hurry. Although more mindful of how loud she spoke, he couldn't make out anything she said with his ear pressed against her backside. Not that he cared what she had to say right now anyway.

She slipped again, and this time her flashlight careened to the ground. At least they were fortunate enough that its dim glow lit the cavernous room. An enormous shadow sped along the corridor wall leading into the room.

He wanted to watch. See if this creature really was invisible. His heart had paused, and a scream tickled at his throat. But he dared not let it out. Instead, he clung to the ladder. He tried not to look and wanted to move, but his grip tightened securing him to this place. This ladder was all he had left to hold him to reality. That became painfully obvious as the fallen light failed, and the darkness below returned.

A hand found his shoulder. When he turned his flashlight upward, it revealed her face. She looked beautiful in this pale light.

Trembling, yet capable of stirring him out of this dreadful state.

Upon reaching the platform, he scanned for something to dislodge the worn wooden ladder.

"Let's get out of here," she said.

"I need something to..."

When he found nothing, he resigned to the only available tool. He stared into the darkness below with no other choice. Kneeling, he pounded the butt of his flashlight against the ladder in an effort to loosen the rusty nails.

A loud *crack* startled him, and for a moment he thought he'd been successful. He braced himself, but the entire platform shook.

It's on the ladder.

A shrill scream erupted from Lilly. She dropped to all fours and crept up behind him. Her fingers were like spider legs creeping around his sides. When they reached his chest, she clung to his back.

The platform groaned with the additional weight dangling from the remnants of the ladder. The platform quaked with each rung the creature scaled. Yet, still he could see nothing.

He hammered the flashlight down on the wood. With each crash the light blinked off before flickering back on.

It won't hold up much longer. He couldn't decide whether he'd been referring to the light or this platform.

Another hammering, but still the ladder didn't give. The same could not be said of the flashlight. The light wavered, producing little more than a warm glow. A putrid smell wafted to him and his hair fluttered in some unseen breath. The creature was so close now.

Adrenaline powering him, he struck the wooden brace hard. Finally the ladder gave.

A rush of wind whipped at his face, as if something had swiped at him and missed. Seconds later everything collapsed into the darkness.

The creature roared, and Kelvin could hear it leaping for the platform. Its desperate cries echoed throughout the cavern after each attempt. If nothing else this indicated it hadn't been successful.

But for how long?

He banged the light a few times against his hand. When it didn't illuminate, he tossed the flashlight aside and grabbed Lilly's hand. He pulled her toward a speck of light in the distance.

Soon the musty aroma dissipated, and so did the roars. He surmised from this that the creature had managed the platform.

A cascade of twinkling stars greeted them as they exited the tunnel. He stared back at the cave. Not that he wanted to see the creature burst out, but he found he could not draw his eyes away due to the anticipation. Because of this he hadn't seen the rocks half-buried in the earth.

He crashed hard against the ground. A strange fragrance enveloped him, sweet and familiar. Jerking his clenched fists away, he stared at them dumbfounded. A single dilapidated flower suffered his grip.

He hadn't noticed these wildflowers earlier. Now, they mesmerized him. Their beauty and smell enticed him. Thanks to his intrusion many of them now had broken stems.

Lilly stopped several yards beyond him. She hadn't done this to wait for him. Her gaze surveyed the departing train. They'd come all this way only to end up late.

His eyes strained on the train as his fist severed one of the flower's petals. He watched it drift to the ground. With it, his grim thoughts returned.

He heard the train whistle and wished circumstances could have been different. As he rose, the creature's growls breached the opening in the mountain.

Watching the train disappear into the night, he brought the flower to his nose before tossing it to the tracks.

Kenneth W. Cain

About the author: Kenneth W. Cain is the author of the *Saga of I* trilogy, *United States of The Dead,* acclaimed short story collections *These Old Tales* and *Fresh Cut Tales,* and the forthcoming collection *Embers.* He lives with his wife and children in Eastern Pennsylvania. You can learn more about his writing at kennethwcain.com

The Painted Universe

by Lee E.E. Stone

Kelvin pressed against the wound as blood seeped around his hands. He tried to focus entirely on Ravon's face, but he found himself constantly glancing down at the blooming blot of red on her dress. The bullet had gone completely through her, and she was quickly bleeding out.

The smell of Ravon's peach perfume was tainted by a slight scent of burnt gunpowder, but it was more than enough to intensify Kelvin's nauseousness and the terror ransacking him.

"Somebody, help!" He called out, pleading, but all the other metro-train riders had fled the deck.

His muscle tightened, his head spun, and he wanted to throw up so badly. But more than that, he didn't want Ravon to die. "Stay with me, baby—*stay with me!*"

The man in the black dress suit looked on in horror at what he had done, the gun in his hand still smoking. Black tears ran down his cheeks as he sobbed. "Oh God...oh God..."

Kelvin did his best to gently lay Ravon down. The salt of her tears as he kissed her cheeks, nearly sent him into an uncontrollable convulsion of rage, but he bit his lip and reigned it in long enough to direct his anger toward the man with the gun.

"It feeds on all of this," the man said, back peddling toward

the edge of the platform. *"It made me do it! You have to stop it!"* He teetered precariously on the edge above the tracks. He gazed down at his feet—at his shadow—"Oh shit! *Help!*"

Kelvin was in no mood to help, nor was he interested in whatever delusions were currently haunting Ravon's killer—no, he wanted to tear the man apart.

He reached out and tore the red, silk tie from the man's neck, flinging it off to the side in disgust, but as he did so, for just the briefest of moments, deep in the back of his mind, he thought he saw the killers shadow detach from the man's feet, and then attach to his own. He shook his head to regain focus, ignoring the absurd sight from his mind.

A train came around the corner, its metal wheels screaming like banshees as the breaks clamped down.

The man stared at Kelvin, and said, *"I'm so sorry, it has you now—don't listen to it!"*

"Don't listen to what?" Kelvin said.

"The shadows!"

The man fell back into the path of the incoming train and was instantly killed. But to Kelvin, it looked like he had been pushed by something that wasn't there.

***

One year later.

Kelvin stared out at the city from his bench, quietly, waiting for the next train to arrive. Anxiety scratched at the back of his mind like a cat wanting out. He shifted restlessly in the shade, pulling his feet in under the bench, away from the sunlight. The heat had reached triple digits today, and he half-expected the train to roll in with a dozen pitchfork toting devils, milling out of the hot subway car, talking shop.

He clutched the bulky yellow folder on his lap, as if to keep it from fleeing the bright, hot summer sun. The title on it, *The Shadowy*

Muse, shifted and shimmered, like ink under a plate of glass. Sweat stung his eyes and his muscles ached from near-constant sitting for the past 8 months as he wrote the manuscript in the folder. The two inch thick stack of pages felt heavier than they should be, easily a pound or two more than it actually weighed, and the entire thing seemed to breath under his hands, like some strange, abstract creature out of a William S. Burroughs' story.

A woman plopped down on the bench next Kelvin, giving him a bit of a fright. He looked at her, and was caught off guard once more, as the sweet smell of her peach perfume tickled his nose. For just a moment, he was staring right at Ravon.

The horn from a train Kelvin hadn't realized had pulled in, washed the illusion of his dead girlfriend away, revealing a young woman, with the beauty of a 1950s pin-up model. Sunlight glistened off her coiled, white halo of hair that wrapped around the crown of her head. She smiled warmly at him before opening up the beige tackle box on her lap, quickly sifting through it.

The folder shifted in Kelvin's sweaty hands, as if trying to get away from the woman.

She looked over at him. "Hi!"

Kelvin's cheeks warmed. "Hello."

"The name's, Em."

"Kelvin." He smiled back at her.

"'*The Shadowy Muse*? You're a writer, right?"

He glanced at the folder. "I suppose."

"You suppose?" she said. "Something on your mind?"

"I'm sorry, do I know you?" He felt, oddly, offended.

"In a manner of speaking," she said.

She did seem familiar, but it was more her presence, than her face, that rang a knowing pang inside him. "Sorry, drawing a blank."

She nodded. "I see, it would appear he's got his hooks in you, pretty deep." She looked him up and down, like someone checking for defects on a used car.

"Say again?"

"I'm going to cut to the chase," she said.

"I would appreciate that."

"I'm a Muse," she said, a song in her voice.

Kelvin chuckled. *This woman is nuts.* "Oooh-kay!"

Em ignored his rude reaction, and her smile faded, replaced with a stern look. "You've been coming here, once a week, for the past 8 months, with that ever-growing story. You sit right there, and stare at the city, as if you're looking for something out there." She went to touch the folder and Kelvin moved it to his other side before she could. "I know there's a presence in it, and it's keeping you from moving on. Stories are dying to get out of your heart, but that black shadow hanging over it is keeping them buried. It's feeding off of them. Off you and all the pain and misery swirling about in there."

How does she know about the shadows? "Her parents sent you, didn't they? They still don't believe me!"

"Believe what?"

"I have to go—"

She grabbed his wrist and kept him from getting up. A warm, electric charge ran up his arm from her hand, and a sense of calm came over him. "Kelvin, if I'm to help you, we need to do this before the sun sets; before the shadows take form."

With a heavy sigh, he relented. "This is crazy—you know what, fine, I'll bite: what do you need from me?"

"Tell me about the story in that folder."

"It's about a writer," he said. "He tries to capture the demon responsible for the death of his girlfriend." He shifted, restless and unsettled, the momentary calming effect Em had over him began to weaken. "Can you help, or not? What are you, some kind of traveling psychologist?"

"Like I said, I am Muse. At any rate, I will most certainly try to help you. Tell me how it all began."

"I met Ravon two years ago at an art exhibit down the street from my apartment. There was a painting of this dream city that kind of looked like New York City at night, but, bigger, more expansive. Anyways, it was called *The Painted Universe*, and it was for sale.

"My writing had hit a wall, and just looking at this exquisite piece of art lit a fire inside me. So, I go into the studio where the painting was and there's this very down-to-earth, girl-next-door looking woman standing next to it, speaking to some people. Blue jeans, paint speckled vintage rock band tee-shirt, black horned rimmed glasses, and hair white as snow, like yours..." He felt the smile come over his face. "Come to find out, she's the artist responsible for the painting and her name was Ravon. I walked over to her, and to my surprise, we hit it off instantly.

"I offered to buy the painting, but only if she went out on a date with me. And time—my god—it went by so fast!

"Fast forward to our two-year anniversary, she's waiting for me here on this bench. I had a ring with me, I was going to propose, so I tried to sneak up on her. But then this guy in a black dress suit shoves me out of the way and starts shooting a gun all over the place. One of the bullets caught Ravon in the gut and..."

"You don't have to go on," Em said.

He shook his head. "No, it's okay." He took a deep breath and looked out into the city. "I grabbed that son of a bitch, but all I got for my effort was his red tie. He went on and on about talking shadows, and whatever—I wasn't really listening to him. I wanted to kill him. I swear, I'm a good man, but my God, I wanted to kill him for what he did to Ravon!"

"What happened to him?"

"He threw himself in front of a train"

"Oh...wow. What happened next?"

"With Ravon gone, I was left to the darkness, and after a

while, I started to hear it speak to me—like how you hear a voice in your head, but you know it's not your own because it feels out of place, and unfamiliar. Yet I listened, and it told me to write, and the more I wrote, the faster the pain would go away. But it never did, no matter how much I wrote. But I knew something it didn't."

"Really? Like what?"

"If I kept writing, it would stay in the book, and nobody else would get hurt. The way I see it, the man in black tried to run, but it just got Ravon and himself killed. It was the demon. It had to have been."

Em rose to her feet. "Come."

"Wait, that's it?"

"Just come with me."

He followed her over to a white, 10' x 10' section of wall along the back of the platform, lingering doubts to her promise still in his mind.

She revealed a small paintbrush with a red handle engraved with a fine gold filigree of branching, lightning bolts, and a small white rose on the gold-rimmed brace. She cupped it in his right hand and then stepped behind him. She reached around his waist and took hold of the hand that held the brush.

"She's been watching over you all this time," she said in his ear.

He became breathless in the moment as a sense of weightlessness came over him, and he felt like he was floating.

Em guided the brush across the white wall in a wide swash, and in its wake, paint miraculously appeared on the board. The colors shifted and changed as a city came into existence on the once blank mural.

"But she needs you to let go, to free yourself from the pain, to move on." She kissed him on the cheek and an electrical charge jolted down into the hand holding the brush, spilling out onto the canvas, creating a night sky full of blue, white, and orange bursts of colors.

Tendrils of paint dripped down the wall like multi-colored

tears, forming silver skyscrapers that lunged up like mighty, giant knights.

Smaller red and brown buildings popped up like mushrooms at the feet of their towering brethren.

A wave of green washed down the city streets, forming pockets of trees and small parks, gardens, and forests around the edge of the metropolis.

Tiny people made of paint moved about like it was just another night out on the town.

Kelvin wiggled free and dropped the brush to the ground. "Oh my God, that's *Ravon's* painting!" He glanced over at Em who fawned at the mural. "How did you do that?"

An unexpected cold wind blew across the platform and day gave way to night, and the city of the real world vanished. The canopy lights came on weakly, casting long, black bars of jittering shadows across the floor. They moved about like the silhouettes of boney fingers.

A searing pain hit Kelvin in the gut.

"Oh, my God! What's happ—"

The folder slipped free and the pages scattered in the wind, falling around him like rectangular snowflakes. He fell to his knees, the impact sending jolts of pain up his legs.

"*Damn you! This one's suffered enough!*" Em screamed.

Kelvin vomited a black, ink-like, viscous substance onto the floor. It spun around on the floor into itself until it had grown to the size of a manhole cover, bubbling like hot tar pitch, and smelling of rotted meat and spent matchsticks.

Em quickly helped Kelvin to his feet. "We have to get into the painting, *now!*"

"What..." Kelvin pointed wildly at the black puddle. "What in the hell is *that?*"

A featureless figure rose up out of the puddle, its wet outer shell quickly solidifying into a man-shaped form. The shell fell away in large flakes of ash, revealing a man in a black dress suit. He had two empty eye-sockets, and a mouth full of black, needle-like teeth.

White puss-like gel seeped out of the two empty eye-sockets, wrapping around the skull to form a gaunt and ghastly looking face like Lon Chaney in *Phantom of the Opera*. Two ruby-red eyes filled in the sockets, rolling out into view like two plump cherries.

A lone tendril of red slime dripped out of the monster's gaping maw, landing on its chest where it took the form of a red dress tie, wrapping around the monsters neck, like a noose. Several hundred lines of text appeared on its head where hair would have been on a human, each letter accompanied by a clacking sound of chattering teeth, sounding like a typewriter.

"That's the monster from my story!" Kelvin said. He stepped in front of Em to protect, unsure if he would be of any use.

Shadow moved with supernatural alacrity behind Em. The thing spun her around to face him, like a ballroom dancer.

"*No!*" Kelvin yelled.

Shadow impaled Em with one of his talon-tipped hands, spilling paint-like blood from her gut onto the floor. Kelvin quickly grabbed her before she fell to the ground. Shadow said nothing as it walked to the painting, cocking its head from side to side, as if turning a mental key in an imaginary lock hidden within the nightscape piece.

"*Why?*" Kelvin screamed.

Shadow turned on its heels to face his interrogator.

Em whispered to Kelvin, "*The painting—*" She let out a long, haggard sigh before she crumbled into a fine, pastel dust in his hands.

He hyperventilated as the granules of Em drifted through his fingers and into the painting, like the white, wispy pedals of a dandelion. He roared at the top of his lungs, straining every last muscle in his body to push out the rage within him.

Shadow took a step toward him, chuckling.

Kelvin got to his feet and swung at Shadow with a left, and then a right.

Shadow's head turned to black mist as Kelvin's fist went right through it. Kelvin swung again, but this time his clinched fist was met by one of Shadow's fists.

He drove Kelvin to his knees before grabbing him by the collar and hoisting him a foot into the air.

"*Truth teeters on the edge of reason,*" Shadow said with a hoarse voice. He pinned Kelvin up against the painting with a hard thump. The fingers of its right hand snaked and stretched unnaturally down to the floor and came back with the brush.

"What are *you?*"

Shadow grinned, his breath sickly, metallic. "*Boogieman, demon, nocnitsa? Who can keep up with all those names?*" He licked at the brush, but quickly withdrew it, a soured look on his face. "*Hope: so revolting.*"

"God, please stop!"

Shadow twisted Kelvin's shirt collar tight, and his eyes exploded with fire inside of them, "*I'm God now!*"

The paintbrush ripped itself free of Shadow's grip, and plunged itself into the painting.

"*What?*" Shadow said.

Kelvin fell back into the painting as if it were water, landing on the other side with a soft thud against a white tile floor. He scrambled to his feet and found himself inside the painting. The air smelled of earthy clays, linseed oil, and strong gasoline-like solvents in the air.

Shadow slammed his fist against the invisible barrier that barred his crossing over to the painted side.

"The wall won't last," said a familiar voice behind Kelvin, one he never thought he'd hear again.

"Ravon? How is this possible?" Kelvin stumbled over to her. "Is that really you? Why are you wearing Em's clothes?"

Ravon smiled. "She helped me get to you, but don't worry about her, her kind are everywhere, and she's not truly gone, as neither am I from your life."

He put his lips to hers—every second of that soft kiss made his body tingle. The moment was electric.

But it was not meant to last.

Shadow broke through the barrier and swooped into the painted world as a swarm of black pages, reforming behind them. He dragged Ravon, kicking and screaming, over to the edge of the platform above the tracks.

"Enough!" Kelvin clinched the brush tight in his hand and spun Shadow around.

The monster glanced at Kelvin's hand and then at Kelvin with a dismissive glare. *"What is this?"*

The brush pulsed bright with a white, crackling energy.

Kelvin grinned as a dismayed look came over Shadow's face.

"*Wait! I gave you the words,*" Shadow said.

Kelvin tore the tie from the monster's neck and threw it onto the tracks. Red mist sprayed in his face from the fist-sized hole in Shadow's throat.

Shadow gasped and gurgled as slurred words in some dead language escaped from his lips. Releasing Ravon, he flailed wildly, grasping at his throat.

Kelvin plunged the handle of the brush between Shadow's eyes, sending a shockwave that blew him back onto his ass.

Shadow teetered on the ledge above the tracks, the light in his eyes flickering off and on, like a pair of red Christmas lights with a short in them.

Kelvin charged back over to Shadow. He kicked the monster with every last ounce of strength he could muster.

Shadow fell down into the train tracks, and quickly got to his feet. He looked up at Kelvin and opened his mouth to say something, but instantly exploded into countless pieces of paper as a train hit him head on.

Kelvin turned to embrace Ravon, but found himself back in his own world, with no sign of her, the painting, or Shadow. The light cast off from the brush in his hands, dulled and then finally disappeared. He watched in silent amazement as it turned into a beautiful white rose. He didn't understand, but chose not to question it.

The folder containing his manuscript felt lighter than before, almost weightless. He scoffed, tossing it into a trashcan as he walked over to the edge of the platform.

A train flew by, and he smiled up at the stars. Watching the train disappear into the night, he brought the flower to his nose before tossing it to the tracks.

About the author: Lee Eguia Elam Stone became fascinated with dark, surreal fiction at the age of 12, when his father gave him a worn copy of Niven and Pournelle's modern spiritual successor to Dante's first book in the Divine Comedy epic, *Inferno*. Ever since then, Lee has been digging through the mine in his mind, in search of the pieces to his own adventures into the dark underworld of the dreamlands, a place he lovingly refers to as the "In-Between."

Worlds Hath No Chance Against A Woman Scorned

by Roxanne Crouse

Kelvin pressed against the wound as blood seeped around his hands. If the black ooze pouring from the alien's arm could be called blood. The gooey substance flowed faster than human blood, and smelled like crude oil, making him gag.

Kelvin pressed harder, doing his best in the dim, greenish light emanating from the parkinglot streetlamps near the field. His heart pounded like a jackhammer as the weird liquid continued to gush from the bullethole. A tightness formed in his chest as his eyes shifted to the wound and to the gun on the ground. Why did the situation have to come down to shooting it?

Kelvin's partner on the recovery mission, Ashley, ran at top speed toward him. The scowl on her face grated his nerves. She skidded to a halt and planted herself next to him in the grass.

"Why did you shoot it!" Ashley choked as her chest heaved. Her sweat-saturated hair clung to her face and neck. She shoved against him, almost knocking his hands from the alien's wound.

"I had no choice! It was headed right for a civilian populated area." Why couldn't she have gotten lost in the dark? Paired together twenty-four hours ago, she cut down his every decision treating him like an imbecile. Her sophisticated degrees apparently made her too good to be partnered with a low-level soldier.

"I saw it stop!" she yelled.

"Yeah! My only opportunity to shoot it! This thing is inhumanly fast. I only shot the arm."

"Nothing but a testosterone bag," she said, rummaging around for something.

Kelvin ignored her, shifting his hands on the wound, trying to find a better position to slow the blood. Blackness continued oozing out as if the creature was nothing but a garden hose.

Ashley heaved her shirt over her head revealing a dingy white bra underneath. She would wear ugly underwear.

His attention snapped back to the alien on the ground. If the thing died, God only knew what the D.O.A.R. agency would do to him.

"We don't know anything about its anatomy! Shooting it in the arm could kill it! The other one died in minutes from a chest wound that would be minor to a human."

"If its so delicate why'd they give us guns to catch it?"

"Because men are idiots and that's all that controls the D.O.A.R., idiot men." She held both ends of the shirt and twirled it in the air until it was long and tight. Shoving the twisted shirt against his arm, she yelled, "Here! Use this as a tourniquet!"

Kelvin grabbed the shirt with blackened fingers, keeping his other hand pressed on the wound. He fumbled around one-handed, working the makeshift tourniquet under the alien's thin arm, and then tied it off fast and tight, so tight he wondered if the alien had bones or muscle under the grey skin. Was the shirt too tight? Kelvin had no way of knowing, but the black ooze slowed.

Fighting off the urge to smooth back his sweaty hair, he smeared the black substance on his camo uniform, though he would rather smear it on Ashley.

Would he contract some strange alien disease? The D.O.A.R.

would probably use the exposure as an excuse to throw him in quarantine for the rest of his life.

"What now?" he asked.

"We send up a flare. The containment unit will come and pick up Mr. Grey."

Kelvin raised an eyebrow. "Mr. Grey?"

"A name the research team gave him."

"How do you know it's a male?" Kelvin asked.

"We don't. The male dominated research team assumes it's a male."

Rolling his eyes, he pulled a flare from his utility belt and set it off. A ball of light shot up toward the dark clouds, exploding like a miniature firecracker. A red glow hung in the air after the other sparks died away. The flare's light cast an eerie red glow on everything. He shivered.

In the lab, Kelvin never saw Mr. Grey up close. His job entailed standing for hours with an M16 and keeping his mouth shut. Once, he got a glimpse of the thing as the scientists transported it from one examination room to another, but a white sheet covered most of the alien and a translucent dome distorted the rest.

He gawked at its motionless body, taking in every detail, finally joining an elite group to see an extraterrestrial up close. Too bad the memory of almost killing it threatened to ruin the moment.

"Is it even alive?" he asked. Close up, the alien's eyes didn't look organic, more like opaque, plastic disks. The black almond-shaped surface didn't reflect light like human eyes and no eyelids. The creature's grey skin felt like soft, damp plastic, the same kind used to make chewy dog toys.

If Kelvin didn't know better, he'd swear D.O.A.R. was trying to pull a fast one on the scientists with a fake rubber alien, but he saw the thing in action. If he hadn't shot its arm, they would have never caught it.

"I don't know. It hasn't moved. Your bullet may have killed it."

Her angry tone stung. The last thing Kelvin wanted was to go down in history as the first human to kill an alien. Besides that wasn't the question he asked. This creature looked synthetic.

"What's this?" Ashley scooted the uninjured arm away from the body.

Kelvin leaned in closer. Something was in creature's elongated fingers.

"Why does it have a flower?" Kelvin asked.

"I don't know. Must be the reason it stopped running." She lifted the creature's arm and examined the plant.

A cluster of small purple flowers began at one end of the long stem. Velvety green leaves sprang out from the base. The alien had pulled out the roots and everything. When Ashley moved the buds up closer, a strong vanilla scent, or maybe even pie scent hit Kelvin's nose, the kind of pie his nana used to bake.

His stomach growled. The alien search had gone on for more than twenty-four hours and he hadn't eaten since it started. "Wow. Strong smell. Why would it stop in the middle of an escape to pick a weed?"

"It's not a weed," Ashley said. "It's a heliotrope, also known as a cherry pie plant. They were popular in the 1900s and almost became extinct until gardeners recently revived an interest in them again."

"Okay." Kelvin dragged the word out. "Why do you know so much about this flower?"

"I'm a biologist, remember?" Ashley pulled her hair away from her face and neck. Her freckled cheeks flushed with red. "Plus, my grandmother grows them."

"What's Mr. Grey doing with it?"

"I don't know."

A-ha! Finally, something Miss Smarty Pants didn't know.

The long, thin fingers clamped the stem like crocodile jaws. Ashley grunted and pulled, but the alien's fingers wouldn't budge. She sighed as if defeated, and then glared at Kelvin. "You want to try?" She shifted her eyes away, uncomfortable.

Kelvin smirked. "Sure." His sneer grew larger as he reached to take the alien's arm from Ashley.

A shrill, stabbing pain engulfed his brain. The alien's arm dropped to the ground. He and Ashley both rushed to cover their ears, but the blare arose from inside, no way to block it. A warm liquid tickled the sides of Kelvin's face and his palms felt warm and wet. He bent to the ground and closed his eyes, praying he'd pass out.

An eternity passed before the throbbing eased and Kelvin could process thoughts again. He didn't dare open his eyes, the pain might return. As he lay cupping his ears, his forehead pressed against the cold ground, pictures began to flash through his mind at a rate he couldn't comprehend. The throbbing threatened to return full force as he tried to slow down the barrage of images. Unfamiliar scenes and emotions rushed in, filling his brain.

Depictions of the alien traveling, crashing, escaping, running. The flower. Images drowned his mind of the purple flower, followed by strong emotions of importance.

The last picture turned his stomach. Acid rose up his esophagus burning his throat. Millions of strange creatures lay dead against an extraterrestrial landscape of reds and greens. The bodies stretched into the distance, disappearing in the light of a blue sunrise.

An overwhelming loss followed, sweeping through Kelvin's body until he trembled and cried. He hadn't felt such sorrow since the death of his nana, the only real mother he had ever known. Pictures of her, stolen from his mind, flashed intensifying the anguish. Her dyed red hair, the same color it was before it all turned grey, and her warm smile as she pushed a pie in the oven. Kelvin believed his heart would burst from the grief when cool hands touched his skin, ripping him from the stream of sensations.

His body jolted. The flashes stopped, but the surreal sorrow lingered in every tissue of Kelvin's being. He stumbled as the dark field, alien body, and Ashley's grabbing hands jerked him back to earth. The shrill pain in his head stopped, but his ears rang with its memory.

"Kelvin! Are you all right? What happened to you?" Ashley's frantic voice grated like a room filled with screaming babies.

"Quiet!" He grasped the sides of his head to keep it from splitting apart. He wanted to hear his nana's voice again.

"Your ears are bleeding!" Ashley tried to wipe the blood with something, but Kelvin elbowed her in the chest. "I'm trying to help you!"

"Please! Leave me alone, I'll be fine." As the ringing subsided, Kelvin's mind grasped at the knowledge the alien gave him, but the impressions slipped away like sand through his fingers.

"Oh, my god!" Ashley yelled. She yanked him away from the body.

Kelvin opened his eyes. Ashley's face had drained of color, the freckles almost invisible. He followed her gaze. The alien was sitting up staring at him with black, plastic eyes. Kelvin recoiled.

The arm holding the flower rose up in Kelvin's direction.

"What's it doing?" Ashley backed away, shaking.

Kelvin's mind shuffled through the images trying to make sense of them, searching for a message, an answer, anything.

"Ashley, listen to me. We need to let him go."

"What?"

"Right now. Before the recovery teams arrive."

"Are you crazy?"

The sound of swishing blades grew louder, helicopters.

"He gave me a message. We need to help him escape!"

"No! No way! You've lost your mind." Ashley yelled over the increasing noise and wind. "They'll throw us in prison, or worse!"

"We have to or millions will die!"

Bright lights fell on them, blinding Kelvin. The wind tossed grass and dirt in every direction as if a cyclone engulfed the entire field. Kelvin fought to stay balanced on his feet.

Worlds Hath No Chance Against a Woman Scorned

The alien stood amongst the chaos, motionless, still holding the flower out for Kelvin as if the winds didn't exist.

"Run!" he yelled at it. "You're free. Go now!"

"No!" Ashley scrambled to the ground grabbing the gun resting next to the pool of black alien ooze. She stood, her hair whipping around her desperate eyes, and pointed the barrel right at Kelvin's head.

"Another fucking male isn't ruining my life!"

"What? Didn't you see the images? We need to let him go!"

"Hands up or I'll shoot!"

The alien turned to Ashley. She paid no attention to it. All her attention focused on Kelvin.

"Didn't he show you?"

"Show me what?" She cocked the hammer, safety disengaged.

"The dying world!" The rotors drowned Kelvin out. Did she hear him? The barrel stayed trained on his head. He had to do something before the alien ran out of time.

The alien's stubby legs nudged toward Ashley, its injured arm reached out in her direction. She backed away, shifting the gun to the creature, her breathing wild.

"Don't shoot it!" Kelvin yelled.

A dart hit the alien's back. While Ashley was distracted, Kelvin jumped and kicked the gun from her hands.

"Run now!" Kelvin yelled, but the alien didn't run. It stopped, its arms lowering to its sides. The flower dropped from its fingers to the ground.

Kelvin dashed for the gun lying near Ashley. She went for it, too, but he pushed her and she stumbled back falling on her haunches.

"Stop right there!" he yelled. He backed up, keeping the gun on her, until he reached Mr. Grey's side. The flower lay below him about to blow away in the hurricane. He reached down and grabbed the stem. Ashley remained on the ground, bewilderment painted her face. Kelvin pulled the dart from the rubbery, grey skin of the alien's back and tossed it to the ground.

Mr. Grey's short legs gave. Kelvin caught the creature before it fell. Something stung his neck.

"Crap!" Kelvin lowered the limp Mr. Grey to the ground, and his own body followed as his limbs went numb. Another dart hit Ashley in the side of the neck. She yanked it out throwing it to the ground.

Seconds later, the helicopters landed. Kelvin's last memory was of bright lights, wind, and scientists surrounding him with guns.

***

Kelvin awoke to a familiar beeping sound. He found himself in the backseat of a sedan, the door hanging wide open letting in the cool night air. The dome light illuminated everything inside the car, blacking out the world outside. His uniform was gone, replaced with a plain white T-shirt and jeans. An envelope lay on the seat. Kelvin picked it up and looked inside. Empty.

On the floor, a bit trampled and broken, lay the purple flower, forgotten. Kelvin grabbed it, and checked the ignition for keys. Gone.

Oh, crap.

The D.O.A.R. had dumped him. Anyone who became high risk was immediately removed from the project, one way or another, and the secret location relocated. He was out of the program for good.

A loud, distant whistle sounded. Kelvin poked his head out the open car door. An old wooden building the size of a small house sat on the far side of train tracks surrounded by an evergreen forest.

Kelvin climbed out of the sedan, making his way to the old station. In front, on a wooden bench waited Ashley, alone, and dressed in civilian clothes instead of scrub pants and a ratty bra. The last person Kelvin wanted to see. Her face twisted as her shoe pounded the cement.

Worlds Hath No Chance Against a Woman Scorned

A train slowly approached the platform, brakes screeching as they released pressure. Kelvin dashed across the tracks and stood in front of her. A cool breeze rustled his back as the train entered the station.

Her stiff posture and frowning lips suggested anger, deep anger. In her hands, she held two tickets. She must have taken them from the envelope. At least the D.O.A.R. didn't abandon them in the middle of nowhere, like Death Valley.

"What happened?" Kelvin asked.

"What's it look like happened? We're out!" She crossed her arms tight, crunching the tickets.

"We have to get back!"

Her eyes narrowed. "There is no getting back. Don't you get it? We're out! They'll change the location. We'll never find it thanks to your stunt. We. Are. Out."

"Mr. Grey gave me a message. I don't know how, or why, but he needs this flower to save thousands, maybe millions. We've got to get it to him and help him escape."

She laughed, a strangled chuckle. "Right. The alien knows English and told you this. How did you ever get picked for this project?"

"No," Kelvin said. "He showed me pictures in my head of an alien world dying."

"Sure he did." Ashley stood and forced one of the crunched tickets against Kelvin's chest. "You men are all the same. You think the world revolves around you. It doesn't!"

The train stopped and Kelvin thought his heart would stop with it. How would he convince her?

"All aboard!" a man dressed in a conductor's suit yelled, hanging from the train.

"I hope I never see you again." She released the ticket against his chest and it fluttered to the ground. She marched up to the conductor, handing him her ticket and tossed Kelvin one last hate filled gaze before boarding the car.

Kelvin stood stunned, the image of thousands dead haunting him. Mr. Grey needed the flower. He needed to escape. How would Kelvin convince the government to help the alien when he couldn't even convince one nut case woman? He'd never get within a hundred miles of the alien's location. Not without Ashley.

He stared at the broken flower, the stem bent, the velvety leaves drooping, and most of the purple petals gone or dying. Ashley called it a cherry pie plant, an easy name to remember. He could think of his nana to remember the name. She baked the best cherry pies in town.

Somehow, he'd help Mr. Grey. Kelvin had no earthly idea how, but he wasn't quitting. He couldn't let millions die. Someone would return for the sedan, and when they did, he'd be there, waiting. No crazy, man-hating woman was going to stop him from saving an entire alien world.

Kelvin let out a deep breath. His mind made up. Even if it cost him his life, he'd help Mr. Grey escape. Somehow, he'd find Ashley and convince her to help.

Watching the train disappear into the night, he brought the flower to his nose before tossing it to the tracks.

About the author: Roxanne Crouse is the author of two short stories available at Amazon. She is currently working on a young adult fantasy trilogy she will self-publish in the near future. As a devoted reader of horror, fantasy, and science fiction, she loves to delve into these different worlds and meld them together in her writing. She lives with her husband, son, and loyal cat in West Virginia and spends the time she's not writing as an artist and self-published book reviewer. www.darkwhimsicalart.com.

Soaked in Blood

by Denise Wyant

Kelvin pressed against the wound as blood seeped around his hand. He also grimaced as other injuries announced themselves—a throbbing pain on his cheek and aches when he breathed deeply. *Nice tumble, Kelvin. Leaving a trail of blood is one way to attract a* chupacabra.

Stephanie's voice floated down to him from atop the hill, "You okay, Kel? I'm trying to find a way down to you."

"Yeah, I'm good," he yelled. Kelvin chuckled at the sound of his nickname. Not long after meeting him, Stephanie shortened his name to Kel. However, the first time he called her Steph, he received a ten-minute lecture on that not being her name. "Take your time—those ferns are covering a bunch of loose rocks." Kelvin shrugged off his heavy pack. Gently setting aside his camera equipment, he found the small first aid kit. *Little underprepared, huh? Skimping on first aid supplies wasn't so smart.*

An "oomph" sounded from his right. Stephanie slid the last couple of feet down the slope on her butt, a shredded vine clutched in her right hand. Pitching the vine, she brushed off her shorts and walked over to him. "How bad?"

He raked a hand through his hair as she assessed him. Stephanie, who practiced law for a living and was a competent outdoorswoman, scanned his upper body before moving to his legs. Her eyes widened slightly when she saw the blood trickling to his already soaked sock.

"Not good, I know." He straightened the wounded leg. "Knee is working fine, but my ankle feels like it's softball-sized."

Stephanie squatted next to the bandages that comprised his first aid kit. "That's all you brought?" She grabbed her pack and retrieved a much larger kit, along with a Swiss multi-tool.

"Glad one of us is prepared." He gave her a crooked grin. "I hope you know how to use it—some of that stuff looks dangerous."

"I don't know about you, Kel, joking when we're deep in the Costa Rican jungle." She glanced at her watch, frowned. Kelvin guessed she was concerned about making it back to camp before dark. He didn't want to be out past sunset either. His goal of capturing a *chupacabra* on film could only be safely accomplished in the daylight.

"My apologies, counselor. I concur; this is a very serious situation." He smothered a laugh.

"Boys." She moved to clean his wound and paused, looking off to his left. "What made those tracks? The claw marks are a good two inches long."

Kelvin glanced at the marks. *Ahh, chupacabra.* "Let's get me bandaged up and get moving."

She disinfected and wrapped the gash on his shin. After repacking their belongings, Stephanie helped Kelvin stand.

"Any idea how to get back to civilization?" He watched her scan the area. They were a good half mile downhill from the trail.

"Why don't you check around to see where we can climb up? I'm going to find a walking stick." After a couple of minutes, he located a sturdy branch that would double as a crutch. He inhaled, filling his lungs with sulfur-tainted air and smiled. The chupacabra was close. He fingered his pack, deciding if he should ready his camera. He opted to wait. "Did you find a path?"

She frowned, pointing to her right. "It's narrow, but relatively smooth."

"Lead the way. I'll be right behind you." He smiled despite the pain that flared in his ankle.

They hadn't hiked very far when Stephanie halted. Kelvin saw the alarm in her eyes when she looked back.

"What's wrong?"

She pointed to a large, dead cat sprawled beside the path. Kelvin's curiosity took over. He lowered himself to examine the animal. When he saw additional tracks and two puncture wounds in the cat's neck, his excitement grew. He held his hand over the jaguar's back. Heat radiated from its body. Kelvin peered into the jungle; he had a feeling they were being watched.

"What are you doing? Those are the same tracks as before, right?" Stephanie asked, suspicion lacing her voice.

He rose to his feet. "Just trying to see what happened, that's all."

She crossed her arms over her chest and lifted her chin. "Why are there more tracks? What made them?"

"Yes, those are the same tracks. They belong to whatever predator took down the cat." He shot her an are-you-happy-now look.

She raised an eyebrow, and Kelvin sighed. He felt badly for withholding information from her. After all, she chose to spend the day with him. He feared her logical mind would have trouble handling the truth. "Have you ever heard of a chupacabra?"

Stephanie nodded. "The mythical creature that preys on farm animals by drinking their blood? Yes, I read the lore when I researched this trip."

This is good. She knows the legend even though she thinks it's a myth. "That would be the one. This jaguar has two puncture wounds in its neck. If I had to guess, I'd say its blood has been drained." *This must be one hell of a large chupacabra to take down a cat.* Anticipation coursed his veins. He barely contained his enthusiasm. *This would be the find of the century.*

"I don't buy it, but whatever. We need to get moving."

The ground shook with a great rumble of thunder. Lightning cracked nearby. Kelvin met Stephanie's gaze. "I'd say we're about to get wet."

"It figures. At least we aren't the tallest things out here." She no sooner finished speaking than the sky ripped opened. Torrential rain pummeled their bodies, stinging their skin.

Kelvin grabbed her arm. "Let's take shelter under those rocks."

By the time they reached the slight overhang, they were soaked. Stephanie tried to wring the excess water from her tank top. Kelvin perched on a rock and elevated his throbbing ankle. They were stuck until the storm passed. He checked his watch. Under the dense rainforest canopy, night would soon be upon them.

He glanced at Stephanie, unable to tell if she wanted to laugh or cry. Reaching out, he took her hand and gave it a reassuring squeeze. "Don't worry. The rain will let up soon enough. We'll be back at camp in time for dinner."

She squeezed back. "I'm not worried, Kel. We're in the rainforest, not like we're going to die of hypothermia now that we're soaked to the bone."

He liked her toughness, her ability to remain calm no matter the situation. *Too bad you can't trust her with your obsession of all things mystical and paranormal. A girl like her would ditch you in a heartbeat. Although the trust fund made you a multi-millionaire, you're a freak. Such a shame, Kelvin, she could tame your unearthly passions and make you into a respectable scientist.*

Bumping his shoulder, she brought him back to the present. "Where'd you go?"

His eyes refocused as he released her hand. "Just thinking about that stupid tumble. I hate moving at turtle speed."

She laughed, a light lilting sound. "Slow and steady, and you'll be fine. Not like I'd leave you to fend for yourself!"

He laughed, too. "Good to know!" He glanced up toward the sky, peeking through the leaves of the trees. "Looks like the rain's about done. Ready for more hiking?"

"Let's do it. I'd like to get some dry clothes on."

He couldn't resist teasing her. "You know, you could strip out of your soggy outfit. I wouldn't complain if you hiked naked."

"Puh-lease, Kel. Give me your hand, I'll help you up." Despite her slender build, the girl was strong. *That's right, she could kick your ass in a fight.*

As they left their refuge, the monkeys started chattering. The sounds held a hysterical edge. The hair stood up on the back of Kelvin's neck. He looked over to Stephanie, who had goose bumps up and down her arms. A high-pitched scream interrupted the chatter. It sounded close, much too close for comfort.

"What was that?" Stephanie scanned the treetops. The monkeys raced away from the eerie scream. If he and Stephanie were smart, they would do the same. Kelvin was torn—he wanted proof the chupacabra existed, but with his injuries he was incapable of protecting them from the creature. *Damn it! You got her into this with promises of lush landscapes and overflowing waterfalls. Now you can't even guarantee her safety!*

Another scream echoed, closer. It reminded Kelvin of Miss Beckett, the nun who taught his fifth grade English class, and the way she scraped her fingernails on the chalkboard.

Reality crashed home. Kelvin's ankle wouldn't allow him to sprint from a chupacabra. His male pride demanded he protect Stephanie since he was less than honest about their goal for the hike. He quickly concluded their lives were more important than a picture of an elusive creature. Kelvin caught Stephanie's hand and jerked her in the opposite direction of the sound. "Come on, run!"

He outweighed Stephanie by at least a hundred pounds, yet the girl was determined to support his weight. His routine became stumbling, falling, and having Stephanie tug him back to his feet.

A loud crash sounded in front of them as branches splintered. The wind picked up, tickling Kelvin's nose with a mix of acrid chemicals and decaying animal matter. He tugged Stephanie to a stop as beady red eyes watched them through the foliage. "Oh, shit," Kelvin breathed.

"Is that…is that one of those things?" Stephanie whispered.

Kelvin merely nodded. *What to do? Back away slowly or get ready for the fight of your life?*

The greenish-colored thing vaulted over some brush, landing on its hind legs not twenty feet from them. Kelvin couldn't believe his eyes. A chupacabra. Matted fur covered its scrawny body while blood dripped from fangs peeking out of its mouth. Those glowing eyes never left Kelvin's. He looked away first, noticing the long dirty claws on its human-like hands. The thing screeched again. Both he and Stephanie flinched.

Knowing he wouldn't be able to outrun the creature, he withdrew his tripod and murmured to Stephanie, "Get ready."

The chupacabra jumped, covering the distance between them in one bound. Kelvin crouched with the tripod cocked behind him, waiting to bat the creature like a baseball. In his peripheral vision, he saw Stephanie withdraw her multi-tool and open the knife blade.

The creature studied them, its spiny tail swishing back and forth across the jungle floor. Its red eyes pulsed. The chupacabra's forked tongue flicked out between its fangs, letting loose a stream of fetid breath.

Kelvin cringed. The smell was worse than day old road kill baking in the summer sun. He watched the creature's nostrils flare as its eyes focused on his leg. It must have smelled his blood.

The thing leapt toward him, claws extended. Kelvin timed the swing perfectly, hitting the creature with a solid strike on the side of its head. His tripod broke into pieces as the thing shrieked and flew backward. It landed cat-like on all fours and cocked its head, seeming to reevaluate the threat Kelvin posed.

Shaking its head, it took to the air again, this time targeting Stephanie. Kelvin lunged to put his body between it and her, but his ankle gave out. He crumpled to the ground. Stephanie raised her left arm, protecting her head. Her right arm slashed at the creature, catching its arm and chest. It howled in pain as blood dripped down its body.

Kelvin wanted to hug Stephanie. *We may just beat this thing yet.* He met her gaze as he grasped his heavy pack in front of his body. He hated to sacrifice his equipment; his camera held sentimental value—a gift from his mother who passed away unexpectedly a month ago. However, better to give up the gift than their lives.

It came again, this time trying a different tactic. The thing bounced over their heads. They turned, and it swiped its claws at Kelvin. He used his pack as a shield, ignoring the sounds of tearing nylon. Stephanie moved to flank it while Kelvin parried its blows. His ankle wobbled, weakening, as the creature continued its assault. Kelvin swung the battered pack and landed a glancing blow to its muzzle. His pack snagged on one of the chupacabra's fangs, ripping the front compartment open. His precious camera spilled to the ground. Kelvin would have cried as the creature trampled the equipment, but he was too busy adjusting his stance. The move kept the creature from slicing open his chest; instead, its filthy claws gouged his arm.

Kelvin cursed his earlier hope. He kicked out his injured leg in an act of desperation, trying to trip the thing, but he ended up losing his balance as his leg glanced off the creature's shin. He fell at its feet and rolled into a ball, covering his head with his arms. He braced himself, waiting for the blow that never came.

Slowly, he peeked out between his arms. Stephanie was toe-to-toe with the creature. She wielded the knife as though it was a sword. The front of her tank was soaked with the creature's blood. "Come on, Steph, go for the killing blow," he said.

She balanced on the balls of her feet, dodging and ducking, looking for an opportunity. Soon, the chupacabra left the soft flesh of its belly exposed. Stephanie thrust the knife in and turned. The creature lurched backward and fell to the ground, muscles twitching. A keening wail sounded, strongly at first but then quieted as the creature languished in pain.

Stephanie gave it one last glance before trotting over to Kelvin and pulling him to his feet. "Let's go. I don't know if that was enough to kill it, but I'm not sticking around to find out."

The journey out of the forest was subdued and tense. Kelvin could tell Stephanie was pissed as she marched silently ahead of him. He hoped the damage between them wasn't irreparable. The more he got to know her, the more he liked her, especially after what he just witnessed. The girl could add MMA fighter to her resume after defeating the chupacabra. He wondered what other talents she had. However, the time for discovering them would have to wait.

They limped, battered and bruised, back to camp well after everyone had gone to bed. Too shaken for dinner and knowing any apology to Stephanie would sound contrived, Kelvin headed to his own tent.

***

Kelvin awoke to sunlight. It heated his tent, making it stuffy and uncomfortable. He automatically reached for his camera, and then remembered the little pieces that remained. *Oh well, at least we're alive.*

He crawled out to the sight of the other travelers eating breakfast. He wasn't feeling social so he headed toward Stephanie's tent, determined to smooth things over. Instead of finding her, he found a neat pile of all her things. *What the hell?* The trip wasn't over for three more days. *Think about it, yesterday was probably too much for her. Hell, it was too much for you.*

"Excuse me, Kelvin…" Stephanie skirted around him to

retrieve her belongings. Not good, he was no longer Kel.

He turned to face her. The apology was on the tip of his tongue but never made it out. "What's up? Why are all your things packed?"

She glared. "If you must know, I'm heading home today. The tour company is making travel arrangements to get me to the nearest town that has a train station."

He scuffed his hiking boot into the ground. *Now or never.* "Look, I'm sorry." He paused. "For not being upfront with you about the hike and risking your life."

She sighed, "Save your breath, Kelvin." Her icy gaze locked onto him. "I feel like my souvenir should be one of those shirts that says, 'I went to Costa Rica, and all I got was a lousy, near death experience.'"

Kelvin cringed. "Let me make it up to you. I'll accompany you to the train station and be at your beck and call."

"That's not necessary. I can take care of myself."

"I know you can. Please, I want to." Kelvin's shoulders slumped. Fixing things with Stephanie before she returned to the States was forefront in his mind.

"I can't stop you." She walked away to load up her things. Kelvin followed, ready to cool the ire sparking under her skin.

***

Traveling to the train station took all day despite making just one stop to admire the pale lavender orchids in bloom. It was late in the afternoon before he managed to engage Stephanie in civilized, almost friendly, conversation. *If I could only get her to smile.*

"Well, it's time…" Stephanie adjusted the bag on her shoulder. The train idled on the tracks while other passengers bid farewell to family and friends.

Kelvin moved into her, risking a loose embrace. She allowed it, but only briefly.

"It won't be the same without you here, counselor, who else is going to have my back in a fight?"

She cracked a small smile. "We did make a good team. Once that ankle heals, you won't need any backup."

Kelvin reached up and took the orchid blossom from behind her ear. He gently smoothed her hair. "Nah, no more fighting for me. I've got some investigating to do. On a human this time."

She gave him a wave before making her way onto the train. He searched for Stephanie in the windows but didn't see her. *That's ok. I'll find her soon enough.*

Watching the train disappear into the night, he brought the flower to his nose before tossing it to the tracks.

About the author: The secret is out! Avery Dawes is Denise Wyant's naughty alter-ego! Two minds in one body! While the devil-may-care Avery enjoys the thrill of writing about the passion between two hunky—and sometimes geeky—men, the more traditional Denise favors the alpha male who can sweep an intelligent and sassy lady off her feet. Regardless of which genre they're writing, they both believe in love and happiness, and in happily ever after—even if their characters have to run the gauntlet to achieve it. Whether relaxing with a cup of coffee just south of the Mason-Dixon line, or staying fit by running or cycling—these two always find time to write and blog. You can find them at https://denisewyant. wordpress.com

Kindlestorm's Anomalous Adventure

by LRH Rendell-Hayes

Kelvin pressed against the wound as blood seeped from his hands.

"That'll teach ya for breaking my heart, you twisted sod!" Narisha said, as she looped around in an attempt to point her tainted fingers at Kelvin once more.

Kelvin stumbled as his heart pulsated in spasms—his breathing became strained and rattled up his chest. He leaped to the middle of the tracks before collapsing into the shadow of darkness.

***

A full-figured woman in a vestal veil studied Kelvin, a look of concern on her face.

"What happened? Why is this historical man in my medical room?"

"They say he was attacked by a woman in black down on the Central Park train lines. He only mutters in and out of consciousness, Mother Superior. He passed out once he travelled somewhere between there to our doorstep."

"Well put him over there next to Mr Mumbles. Perhaps between the two of them, we'll get some story one day. What would a woman be doing up on the Central Park tracks in the dark? Perhaps she's a black widow seeking prey," the nun said, as she peered under Kelvin's torn clothing.

The nurse shrugged. "Unsure, but she's sliced a huge chunk in his chest, and whatever did the slicing had a coating of hallucinogen, he's been out of it."

***

Later that day Kelvin jittered from under his bed covers, his eyes sprang open. "She snapped my wand!" he shouted as he slowly regained consciousness.

He scanned the room before trying to regain composure.

"I feel rather lightheaded. Who might you be and what have you done?"

"Oh that's all right, love. We'll have you sorted out in a jiffy," the nurse said as she tucked him in. Kelvin let out a frustrated huff.

"The Doctor will be in later to see if you need surgery."

"Surgery! Where, where's my wand?" he said, nearly falling out of bed. "I had it! It was just busted in two."

"Calm down, I'm your nurse, Mia. Now what good is a wand if it's broken, Kelvin? That's your name, isn't it? And how many fingers am I holding up?"

"You're holding up two fingers, young lady, and yes, Kelvin is my name, well in the mortal realm really. I'm known as Sir. Kelvin Kindlestorm. I was granted a knightship for continual service by Lord Charcolstone himself," Kelvin said, grasping at his stomach, certain his wand was on him somewhere.

The nurse rolled her eyes.

"Of course you were, honey. Tell it all to Mr Mumbles, next door. It'll make you feel better getting it all off your chest."

Kelvin parted the curtain and noticed a thin scale of the man in their shared room.

"Indeed, it appears I'm not in the right realm."

"Realm? This isn't a realm," the man in the neighbouring bed said. "It's our room at St. Teresa's Private Hospital, and I'm Midley, not Mr Mumbles at all." He glared at the nurse as she exited their room.

"I was sent here by the forces of good after all," Kelvin said, rising from the bed.

"It's a pleasure, I'm sure, my fine sir. However, right now I need to find my overcoat promptly and depart."

"They put your clothes over there in that cupboard. Leave here? You've got to be kidding! Have you not seen the state of your chest?"

"Never mind that! My only concern is this dreaded operation. I must leave!" He opened the wardrobe door, finding his jacket, pants, and the broken black wand.

"Here he is, it is sadly snapped but with a little healing, he'll be okay."

"Don't tell me you're talking to that bit of timber," Midley said.

"No, it is not timber. He is my wand that that miserable delver of black magic damaged, because I could not retaliate to her evil ways." Kelvin stared out the window, his mind wondering on the fight he'd had with Narisha, side-tracking his task.

"Yes, well, I'd say you've lost me now, Kelvin." Midley sipped a glass of water, and took three pills by his bedside.

"Give me that!" Kelvin said.

"This?" Midley handed his glass.

"Yes, pass it to me now, and I'll show you what all the four elements are truly about.

Kelvin tousled the water over his carefully positioned wand.

"Elements?"

"Yes, elements: earth, wind, fire, and in our case, ice. Now give me a match."

"They don't keep matches in here, we're in a hospital."

Kelvin whispered to his wand, "Trumdalarah till da'sands of time, come again."

Up burst an open flame that scorched over a stone ice in casement of Kelvin's wand pieces. When the fire faded, it was covered in ice.

Kelvin relished in the look of sheer amazement on Midley's face.

"What's with the fire and ice?"

"I see you've never met a Warlock with my substance. The fire will melt the ice, returning my completely restored wand to perfection.

"I just saw it under that flame…those sands of time are in your wand!"

Midley laughed whilst hugging his pin-stripped pyjamas. "Magic is real?"

"Indeed, but you must respect it. Now for a test!" Kelvin reached into an opening in the newly materialised encasement and cradled his wand like a newborn.

"Heal your maker, Trumdalarah!" Kelvin commanded as he pointed his wand at his wound, which magically transformed his torn flesh to how it was before he'd met with Narisha.

Midley shifted his gaze to his own knees.

"Can you fix me? If you could I'd be ever so grateful."

Kelvin pointed his wand at Midley.

"Restore those non-functioning limbs and make this old Midley of use once more, Trumdalarah!"

As if a fire had caught under him, Midley jumped to his feet; wobbling he smiled, and then danced around on his new legs. "I'm so happy, just thrilled!"

One of the nurses called in from the corridor.

"What's going on, you two?"

Kelvin quickly closed the curtains. "We're fine, just dandy!"

"Well the Doctor will be in to check on you soon," the young nurse said as she closed the door.

"I need to go." Kelvin waved his wand around, drawing grey, swiling smoke, which immediately dressed him.

"Fliddle sticks, I'm going with you!" Midley said, leaping into the cloud.

Kelvin and Midley were magically transported into the dark world that existed somewhere between here and there, in the underworld known to the craft.

"I can't be seen with a mere mortal!" Kelvin said.

"I couldn't stay back there, not now that I know about magical things."

Kelvin rubbed the top of his forehead to fight off the headache. "Fine! But if you're here, you'll plain and simply have to be portrayed as my help."

Midley nodded. "I'm a little unsure if being altered is a good or bad thing."

"We will see what will unfold," Kelvin said. He waved out his wand. "Trumdalarah, vest me thy servant."

This magically transformed Midley into a lanky, teenaged Widget, an elf-like creature with wide, pointy ears, an elongated head, and overly large eyes.

Midley looked.

"There, now you'll blend in, my new minted Midley. We shall go to the Knott's and Trott's Bar and seek out Narisha. She'll be sorry she messed with the likes of Sir. Kelvin Kindlestorm."

"That sounds kinder dangerous, Kelvin."

"Master. You must call me *Master*. Remember Widgets are crafty beings that also share a bout of their master's power."

"Yes, Master. I'm most grateful. What magic do I possess?"

"Mischief and pranks, mostly. In time it will reveal itself. What about family waiting for you, Melvin?"

"No family, I'm an orphan," Melvin said.

"Then a real Widget for good you will be if you wish to serve me. I definitely can't be responsible for you if you're out on your own. You never know who could pick you up."

"Oh yes, then you keep me, Master. I'm thrilled, I can walk!

Kelvin laughed as they talked outside the bar on the corner of Oaks and Notly, in the south side of Maine, just before they entered the establishment.

"Stay close, my young Widget. Things are not always as they appear in a place such as here."

"Well if it isn't Sir. Kelvin Kindlestorm. We haven't seen you in years." Came the voice at the door.

Midley looked around. "Who's talking? I can't see."

"Be quiet, my young Widget. He's new, just over keen to assist." Kelvin said, nudging Midley.

"Do come in with your Widget, Kindlestorm. What can we do for you?

The door opened and Kelvin and Midley entered into a midst of a magical shuffling of goods.

Midley blinked. "Can I draft magic like that?"

Kelvin smirked. "It's not draft, it's cast, Midley. He turned back to the door. "I see your potions and lotions are still sorting themselves precisely, Voice.

Our emporium suffered a break-in and they're doing self-sorting stocktake." The door closed.

"Now, Voice, I'm in search of Narisha, that unnerving Bruja and cast-a-bout. Have you seen her? We've had a mere squabble."

"You two had a fight! Brujo's and Bruja's are forbidden to exchange destructive blows in our midst. Besides I haven't heard her around with that high-pitched tone in her voice.

"As the voice at the door, you must know I always carry my wand with me."

"Ask the Potion Tender at the bar, he talks to all the good sorts in here."

"Thank you, Voice." Kelvin nodded at the large door and then made his way toward the bar.

Melvin ran behind on his new lanky legs, like a weirdly proportioned still growing schoolboy.

"He is the voice at the door, like mortals I believe use a bell? I don't want to talk about this any longer, Midley. Stand behind."

"We've got potions of all sorts today. What can I get for you, Sir. Kindlestorm?" the four handed tender inquired.

"I'm after a potion of truths, and I'll take a bunch of your best roses to boot." The Tender nodded before walking away.

Midley scratched his head. "Roses...blossoms for?"

"Wait, my young Widget. You'll see, now back and be silent," Kelvin replied while looking to see if Midley had drawn attention.

"Here it is, Sir. Kelvin.

"That's Kindlestorm! My master's name is Kindlestorm."

"He's new and a touch overprotective," Kelvin said to the tender. "Next, he'll be sorting my mere dark realm existence."

"Say no more. Anything else?

Kelvin slid a coin toward the multi-limbed tender. "Have you by chance heard where that loathsome, Narisha might be?"

One of the tender's hands snatched the coin up. "Word is she's been trolling the train station."

Kelvin frowned.

"She'd be looking for me. Thank you, Handsel."

"Come along, Midley."

Midley stared at the dark shady creatures looking about, as the Potions Tender handed him twelve red roses and the Truth Potion.

"Whatcha staring at, Widget?" a creature with mystifying features spoke out as he tossed a slice of his jelly flesh in Midley's face.

"Just walk away, Midley," Kelvin said. "He only multiplies once he slices himself."

"No, that hit my head!" Midley took a step towards the culprit.

"Control yourself, Midley!"

Midley pulled back and glared at the smirking splodge. "I'm gonna get you!"

"I'm shaking in my slime, Widget!"

"Come on, Midley, you haven't tested your powers yet," Kelvin said, tugging at Midley's arm. "He's bad news."

Midley stopped and turned back, glaring at the smirking wobbling blob.

"I'm gonna get you!" Midley yelled out. "You slapped me with slime, you slobbering fool!" He stretched out his hand and then pointed at his stomach.

"Midley, you're glowing like hot coals against a fire on a cold winter's night."

"Here's a piece of me, I insist!" He reached into his shirt, and tossed a handful of hot fire balls at the now unravelled blob.

"I'm dissolving, somebody stop that hot tempered widget."

"Yeah…who want's a chunk, slice or cut? I'm an explosion waiting to burst your thirst."

The accompanying creatures, haulted and fell silent.

"NO!" The splodge exploded into a shower of goo, and melted away.

"Midley doesn't disobey!" Midley squealed.

"We must depart." Kelvin grabbed Midley, leading him to the door. "One more casualty, we'll be seen as disturbing the clientele." Midley nodded and followed his master, out of the meeting place.

Once outside, and a block away, Kelvin turned to Midley. "The next time I tell you to desist, you better well do such!"

"Sorry, Master."

Kelvin patted Midley's shoulder and winked with a grin.

"Neat trick! I didn't know I could do that, what was that anyway?"

"Now, Midley you're obviously a widget of our four elements... wind, fire, ice, and stone. You're a force to be reckoned with. You see, a Warlock's widget is only as strong as the warlock he serves, and while you serve me, you'll enjoy a strong bout of power."

***

The pair walked outside The Potions Bar on the corner of Oaks and Notly, and headed straight up a side alley.

"Now, Midley, it will be sometime until your powers fully evolve. I'll need to teach you."

"Okay, Master. I'm all ears!"

"Think of a lovely lady, pretty and noble looking."

"Well there was that one in the hospital." Melvin's form suddenly shifted, and he morphed into the nurse from the hospital. "My name is, Mia!"

"Perfect!" Kelvin Applauded.

"Whoa!" Midley said.

"Well, it's time, let's seed our witch!" Kelvin said, taking hold of the buxom version of Midley.

Smoke enshrouded them whilst they swept away to the tracks, where Kelvin had fought with Narisha.

"Wow, I must say, I do look dazzling. I will sit here, smack bang on the train lines." Midley said, as he admired his new ladylike attire.

"Oh, take a peep at you. Stay here, and plea for me to return," Kelvin said as he became transparent to allow Midley to do the alluring.

"Oh, Kelvin, how I miss you. Why is it so? What will become of me." Midley sobbed, plucking roses from the bouquet.

"I must take this potion you'd given me, for us to be together in all realms of time." Midley took the lid off the smoking concoction and aired it two paces around his standing vicinity to allow the sweet allure to mist about.

The clouds darkened and a fog came over the trainyard as Narisha approached through the opening.

"And who might you be, exactly, young mortal girl with The Realm of Life Potion?"

Her nose was pointy, her hair greasy and heavily matted. "You can't believe what potion delvers tell you these days. We all have to look after ourselves, dearie. Now give it to me, before you hurt yourself, Mortal."

"I can assure you, I am no longer mortal." Midley glanced down at the potion in his pocket.

"He left it for you? That potion's for me and if you won't willingly give it, then I shall take it. You'd be wise to consider that forewarning, my beautiful one."

"No. I'm not a mere woman, you vastly unflavoursome witch! I'll give you a blast of my power. Messing with me, no I don't think so." Midley shook his head in a disapproving manner before transforming and discharging a bout of his steam, hitting Narisha directly in the face.

"Ouch, that was hot! Why you're a four seasons widget, of course! Now where is your Master?"

Narisha started smelling about whilst restoring her face. "Now, I need a mirror!"

Kelvin stepped out of the shadows and onto the tracks.

"Why, it's Kindlestorm," Narisha said.

Kelvin's wand expelled a powerful ball of energy that pulled several bolts of lighting down from the sky, striking the sides of Narisha.

"Oh, so you want to make me dance a touch, do you? Well I can work lightening, you know." Narisha said as she cast out a blast of light directly at Kelvin.

"Now, Widget, give me that potion!" Narisha said, stepping closer to Midley.

The two of them tugged on it until it finally shot into the air and exploded, showering the two.

"See what you've done? So much for The Realm of Life Potion," Narisha said.

"It was not me, it was you," Midley said.

"Why, you're not a Widget! You're a little old man. Look at me."

"Indeed, it was a Potion of Truths," Kelvin said.

"Don't you see what casting back magic has done?"

"So, I'm supposed to cast spells for the good of warlock and man!" She spat on the ground in disgust.

"I can see you need help, Narisha. I failed you once, letting you take your own path, but not this time."

Midley turned to Narisha. "You were his student?"

"More than that," she said with a sneer. "We shared precious moments. Thinking sadly that I was special. So I turned nasty."

A quiver trembled through Midley, upon the tracks.

"Oh my...you're not so tough, Widget. What is that racket?" Narisha said.

"Watch out! That train is coming fast down these lines, and you two are almost human." Kelvin pulled out his wand in a gruelling attempt to protect the now young and innocent Narissa, along with his quivering Midley.

"Trumdalarah, between the tracks!" Kelvin cast out his wand and instantly they disappeared under the cover of darkness.

***

A wandering stranger stepped up, blinking his eyes, as if he'd seen some apparition. He collected one of the roses.

"No way...who would believe me? I saw a magical duel, on the south bound train lines," The man said in amazement.

Watching the train disappear into the night, he brought the flower to his nose before tossing it on the tracks.

181

LRH Rendell-Hayes

About the author: LRH Rendell-Hayes resides on the south coast of Australia. Her father a retired magician, performed under the stage name Dovellini. This is where she first learnt about 'out of the box magical things,' which has evolved into her writing. From childhood LRH has had a passion for light and colour, fantasy and storytelling, with enchanting and detailed images flowing freely from her insightful imagination, as she dream casts a cascade of ideas into type format. She finds the early morning hours the best time to write, and uses the night to work on her upcoming fantasy novel, amongst over projects. Her interests are varied and include, piano, archery, scenic strolls, reading and writing. She particularly enjoys reading fiction generating a magical angle, time travel, supernatural and ghostly adventures. Connect via your Facebook, Twitter or Instagram account to - LRH Rendell-Hayes.

About the Editor

MICHAEL KNOST is an author, editor, and columnist of science fiction, fantasy, horror, and supernatural thrillers. His Writers Workshop of Horror won the 2009 Bram Stoker Award® for superior achievement in nonfiction in Brighton, U.K. His critically acclaimed Writers Workshop of Science Fiction & Fantasy came out in 2013. His debut novel, Return of the Mothman was a finalist for the Bram Stoker Award® for superior achievement in first novel. The Horror Writers Association recently honored Michael with the prestigious Silver Hammer Award for his work as their mentorship program chair. He resides in Chapmanville, West Virginia with his wife, daughter, and a zombie goldfish. To find out more, visit www.MichaelKnost.com.

From Bram Stoker-Award-winning Michael Knost

Softcover ISBN: 978-1-941706-27-5
eBook ISBN: 978-1-941706-29-9

Author's Guide to Marketing with Teeth is a collection of essays and interviews on marketing and advertising for authors and books. Michael Knost has spent more than a quarter of a century in marketing, working in the radio, television, and newspaper industries, as well as serving as marketing director and chief marketing officer for several large companies, including those in the automotive industry.

Mr. Knost has taken the lessons he's learned from his extensive experience and captured the best tips and advice for authors (or anyone in the publishing industry) who hopes to increase sales and/or name brand recognition. Each chapter covers a different subject with tips on theory and execution.

And let's not forget the interviews. Michael is also including several with successful authors to learn about their personal marketing strategies—from when they began their careers to now. You'll hear from superstars such as Charlaine Harris, Diana Gabaldon, Jonathan Maberry, Kevin J. Anderson, Lucy A. Snyder, and Dan Poynter.

From Bram Stoker Award-winning Michael Knost!

Softcover ISBN:
978-1-937929-61-9
eBook ISBN:
978-1-937929-62-6

Writers Workshop of Science Fiction and Fantasy is a collection of essays and interviews by and with many of the movers-and-shakers in the industry. Each contributor covers the specific element of craft he or she excels in. Expect to find varying perspectives and viewpoints, which is why you many find differing opinions on any particular subject.

This is, after all, a collection of advice from professional storytellers. And no two writers have made it to the stage via the same journey-each has made his or her own path to success. And that's one of the strengths of this book. The reader is afforded the luxury of discovering various approaches and then is allowed to choose what works best for him or her.

Featuring essays and interviews with:

Neil Gaiman, Orson Scott Card, Ursula K. Le Guin, Alan Dean Foster, James Gunn, Tim Powers, Harry Turtledove, Larry Niven, Joe Haldeman, Kevin J. Anderson, Elizabeth Bear, Jay Lake, Nancy Kress, George Zebrowski, Pamela Sargent, Mike Resnick, Ellen Datlow, James Patrick Kelly, Jo Fletcher, Stanley Schmidt, Gordon Van Gelder, Lou Anders, Peter Crowther, Ann VanderMeer, Joh Joseph Adams, Nick Mamatas, Lucy A. Snyder, Alethea Kontis, Nisi Shawl, Jude-Marie Green, Nayad A. Monroe, G. Cameron Fuller, Jackie Gamber, Amanda DeBord, Max Miller, Jason Sizemore.

Appalachian Gothic! Jason Sizemore's Irredeemable!
18 Tales of dark fantasy, science fiction, and horror

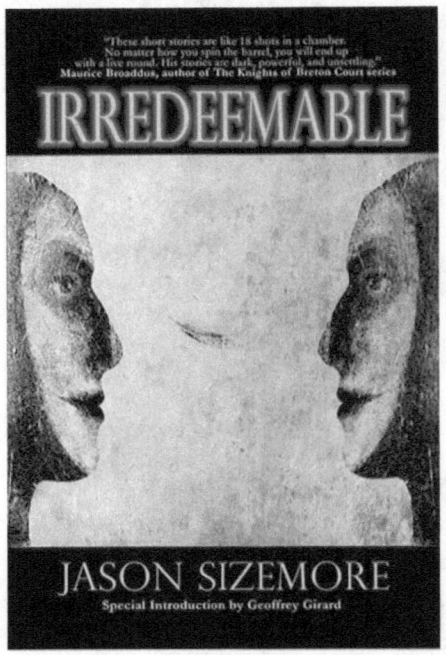

Softcover: 978-1-937929-59-6
eBook: 978-1-937929-68-8

Flowing like mists and shadows through the Appalachian Mountains come 18 tales from the mind of Jason Sizemore. Weaving together elements of southern gothic, science fiction, fantasy, horror, the supernatural, and much more, this diverse collection of short stories brings you an array of characters who must face accountability, responsibility, and, more ominously, retribution.

Whether it is Jack Taylor readying for a macabre, terrifying night in "The Sleeping Quartet," the Wayne brothers and mischief gone badly awry in "Pranks," the title character in "The Dead and Metty Crawford," or the church congregation and their welcoming of a special visitor in "Yellow Warblers," Irredeemable introduces you to a range of ordinary people who come face to face with extraordinary situations.

Whether the undead, aliens, ghosts, or killers of the yakuza, dangers of all kinds lurk within the darkness for those who dare tread upon its ground. Hop aboard and settle in, Irredeemable will take you on an unforgettable ride along a dark speculative fiction road.

Now Available from Seventh Star Press,
the horror stylings of
Michael West!

Trade Paperback ISBN: 9780983740209
eBook ISBN: 9780983740216

Trade Paperback ISBN: 9781937929718
eBook ISBN: 9781937929725

Trade Paperback ISBN: 9781937929954
eBook ISBN:9781937929831

Trade Paperback ISBN: 978-1-937929-18-3
eBook ISBN: 978-1-937929-19-0

Hellscapes, Volume 1
Venture through the infernal, where angels
fear to tread!

From Stephen Zimmer, a new horror
series set in realms where the inhabitants
experience the ultimate nightmare!
softcover ISBN: 978-1-937929-36-7
eBook ISBN: 978-1-937929-37-4